SHADOWS

Helen Mathey-Horn

Cover Designed by Michael Roper

This book is a work of fiction. Names, characters, places, and incidents either are products of the author's imagination or are used fictitiously. Any resemblance to actual persons, living or dead, events, or locales is entirely coincidental.

Helen Mathey-Horn
Visit my website at www.helenmatheyhornbooks.com

Printed in the United States of America

ISBN- 9781731313935

CONTENTS

CHAPTER 1

Maru shivered slightly in the breeze on the lookout hill. For summer in the south it was unseasonably cool. The brisk wind from the west was chilling, despite the sun. She watched her two younger siblings darting to and fro unfettered from castle protocols. When her stepmother had asked her to watch Merl and Myra, she had quickly agreed. The first place she had in mind to take them was to the highest point within the castle mount, the grass fields of the lookout. No one would object to her taking them to the place. Guards were permanently stationed here so there was no danger. The area was spacious enough for The Silnik's children to run to their hearts content. And, Maru could think without interruption.

She kept an eye on the twins' blonde heads as she thought. Well, she did think, but just being in the space granted her room to 'run' also, if only in that her visual horizons spread out in all directions around her and the claustrophobic walls of the family rooms down at the palace level were forgotten.

She turned her head to the east and the open sea. A few ships could be spotted. She wished she had thought to bring a spy glass. To the south more sea, ships and clear skies. She did not bother with the north, it was green jungle and of little interest to her. To the west, however, only a few ships could be seen. She tried to determine who or what they were by the color of their sails. She finally judged them by their size to be mostly her father's warships on patrol. Scattered clouds dotted the far horizon.

Below her position lay the family domicile, then The Silnik's official chambers and jurisdictional rooms, then beyond the castle walls was the city of Grantoli, with buildings that stepped down every prominence and rock right to the harbor. To the south, a rocky outcrop curved south then west to be met across a gap by a matching headland from the north. Directly north towards the jungle side above the marshy water that connected Grantoli to the mainland proper, the houses were more ramshackle and built on stilts to avoid the things that lived in that soggy land and to avoid monthly flooding. At the very highest tides, the city became a virtual island. Below the city were the docks lining the natural harbor formed by the peninsular arms. Maru studied the ships that were anchored. The warships that were in port were easily determined by size, freshness of paint and their secured white sails. Many of the other ships were of the middling merchant class and then smaller still the fisher-folk craft. She looked for *The Laughing Dolfer* due in today and found it. It had its own permanent berth in the area reserved for royal craft. She should see her cousin, Tranin, and uncle, Traru, at dinner. Her uncle, while a silnik, wasn't royal, but as his sister, Maru's mother, had been the mate of The Silnik, he was granted honors.

She thought again about how to word the request she wished to put before her father. Would he let her? Surely there would be no harm? She knew her father and step-mother had been arranging to find her a mate, no simple thing for The Silnik's eldest child, but they would let her have one last wish, would they not? It might even be an advantageous skill to sell to a prospective mate. She was from sailor stock, she should at least be able to sail and navigate a small craft, should she not?

It seemed so reasonable to her that she should take lessons from her Uncle Traru, to know how to navigate and sail. Girls and women used to, it had not been that unusual once, before it was banned. Her father of course would worry about pirates. But to the south or east it would be safe enough and this close to Grantoli the ravens of the waves did not raid for fear of the same sails she could see dotting the water from the northwest around the southern blue horizon to the northeast.

She would be down on the docks now, chatting with silniks and sailors alike, except a year ago her stepmother said it was unseemly for The Silnik's daughter. Unseemly was what she had said with her lips, but Maru could see a different message in her eyes, one of fear. Maru would have laughed, but her father and her uncle had agreed. They did not seem to understand that she had to feel that salt spray on her face or not feel alive. Or perhaps they had, for her father had been apologetic when he told her no.

On a boat with her uncle and cousin, that had to be okay. Just once and then she would go off to some silnik's island enclave and run his household and have their children and die of boredom, except there didn't seem to be a suitable silnik found yet.

Maru was brought out of her thoughts by a sharper chill that made her realize she was still staring to the west. A darkness raced across the water like the shadows of predatory birds. Maru was so surprised she looked up to make certain there were no birds in the sky. The clouds raced on a front that pushed the cool air in front of it. The flags on the poles atop the mount snapped as they changed direction with the incoming winds.

"Merl, Myra, time to go in," she shouted as the clouds darted across the open water headed straight for her position.

The twins stopped their game and noticed the wind. They hurried to where Maru stood on the uppermost edge of the hill. She pulled them close, shivering as the cloud shadows poured through the opening to the harbor. Some overran the hills on either side. They flew across the harbor, streamed over the harbor's docks and raced up the hill at her position. When they crossed her spot blocking the sun, she felt as if she had been physically assaulted. The air temperature, already cool for summer, dropped several degrees and her hair whipped back from her face as the winds of the front reached her spot.

"Maru," cried her brother Merl tugging on her hand.

She looked down at her charges. They both looked up at her with worry in their young eyes.

"Maru?" said Myra more cautiously.

"What Myra?" she asked the girl.

"What shark?" asked Merl.

"Shark?" she asked puzzled.

"You said the sharks were coming," replied Myra with worry in her voice.

"Did I? When?"

"Just now," answered Myra.

Maru shivered. "Time to go," she said with a smile. "Your mother will want you to bathe before dinner." Get them inside, thought Maru. Get them inside, now.

The harbor life moved at the same pace as usual, but Maru could not help feeling that the only safe place for her siblings was in the castle proper. As for herself, she still was chilled with fear of what was coming.

* * *

CHAPTER 2

A maid had taken the two children to clean and change for dinner. Maru passed her parents' rooms in hopes of finding her father alone. She stopped as she overheard their voices.

"Traru had no success?" Her step-mother's voice sounded disappointed.

Her father must have shaken his head for she heard no sound in response to the question.

"There must be someone suitable, Mertin. Maru is a wonderful young woman, someone will be very happy living with her."

"You know it is not as easy as finding a decent or pleasing man," sighed her father. "If they do not suit," he sighed again, "I was lucky, Jazmin. First Maru's mother and now you. It is not often a silnik finds a suitable mate, let alone two in his lifetime. I would like Maru to be happy, to have a family."

"And Traru comes back completely empty handed?"

"He met with the prospects that we had heard of, but no, none of them will do, he says."

"The prospects we had heard of," picked up Jazmin, "Did he hear of any new ones?"

"There are always new silniks arising from their selection by the sea. Yes, he heard of one called Bacher, but the man seems to have no given port."

"What kind of sailor name is Bacher?" asked the woman. "That's a northern name, a lander name."

"It means bear in one of the north tongues, I believe. But he sails the southern seas. I will see what we can find out about him. But I worry…there are silniks among the pirates, what if?"

"Surely not," cried Jazmin. "How could the dolfers choose such men?"

"As no one understands how the dolfers choose," Maru could hear a touch of humor in his voice, "how can we know why they would choose from among the pirates?"

"Like to like," said Jazmin firmly. "I cannot abide the idea that Maru would have a mate who did not match her depth of caring and love."

She heard her father's sigh. "I wish I could be so certain, Jazmin."

Their conversation broke off and Maru decided she should move away to her rooms. This was not the moment to speak with her father. However, if there was no silnik to hand fast on the horizon, then perhaps he would be amenable to her learning to sail. There was time, even if only a month. She could learn a lot. Everyone said she was a quick study.

She pulled at the utilitarian cotton sarong that had made up her dress for the day. It had not been warm enough even with the wool cape for the exposed lookout mount. However, within the castle walls it was much warmer, so Maru cleaned and decided on a white silk rectangle edged in green and folded it for her skirt. She found a green silk top covered with gold embroidery that wrapped tightly around her torso and draped across her left shoulder to hang to her waist. She brushed out her wind whipped hair. The straight blonde strands had darkened some since she had stopped visiting the docks, it was a buttery yellow now as opposed to the almost white it had been. Her skin was paler also. Most sailor folk were bronzed skinned with sun bleached blonde hair. Eyes could vary, but were seldom brown, that seemed to be a trait of those that lived in the lands further to the north.

Maru's were brown. Her mother's had been brown while her father's were a traditional sailor blue. Uncle Traru's were once brown she reflected. She should ask him sometime about her ancestors on her mother's side of the family, the Trawn.

The dinner bell would sound soon. She didn't want to be late if she was to ask her father favors. Her gold cloth slippers made little sound on the floors as she headed for the dining room. It was the first night of the week, so there would be guests. It was one reason she had taken extra care to dress. She had to demonstrate her maturity with the various people that might be included at the table with The Silnik. Afterwards, she would see if she could ask her father for the chance to sail.

"Hello, Minnow!"

Maru turned at the greeting. "Tranin! I saw Uncle's ship in port."

The young man clasped her hand in greeting and then hugged her. His hair was whiter than when she had last seen him. His teeth gleamed in his tanned face as he smiled at her. He wore a blue kilt with a gold trim and a white linen vest open down the front and the red sash of a silnik.

"And what is new, cousin?" he asked still smiling warmly.

"I should be asking you," she said taking his arm as they walked towards the dining room. "Nothing happens in Grantoli and certainly nothing happens to me."

"Count yourself lucky," he said more soberly.

Maru casually looked around before she asked her question, "The pirates?"

"The sea is a big place," he said softly, "It is hard to contain them."

They walked the length of the hall and stopped outside a door. On the other side of the opening they could hear the gay chatter as guests greeted each.

"Tranin, I'm going to ask my father to go to sea."

The young man frowned, "Maru, you are a woman, and this is not a good time."

"Tranin, there will never be a good time. I know your father did not find me a mate. If not now, then it may be never. I have to do this!"

Tranin was still frowning.

"What if a mate is never found for me? Then what? I could be a silnik, I know I could call the dolfers. If I have some experience at sea, then perhaps I could have a ship and..."

"Minnow, you are a woman, and The Silnik's daughter. You forget your father banned women from sailing. You are never going to be allowed to sail."

"If I were a son I would be allowed."

"Maybe," hedged Tranin cautiously.

"I'm going to ask for sailing lessons with your father. The Silnik himself could not protect me more. I'm a sailor, I need to sail."

Her cousin shook his head. "I doubt your father will let you."

They entered the room slowly. Maru had a gracious smile for each person as she moved through the room greeting people she knew and meeting the few that she did not. She looked for her uncle. She spotted him across the room. He was not as tall as his son. His white hair was done in thin braids. One of the maids must have done it for him, she decided. He wore a white linen kilt and vest with a red sash of a silnik. When she met up with him she gave him a formal handshake and then hug.

"Uncle Traru, it is good to have you back in port."

"Do you know you resemble your mother more each day?" he asked.

"How can you say that?" laughed Maru.

"One does not need sight to see the reality of a person," said the man. He turned his milky eyes as if searching the room. "Where did my son get to?"

"He's making eyes at one of the guests," whispered Maru.

"Petit, with a scar on the back of her left hand?" asked her uncle.

"Yes," said Maru. "Who is she?"

"Someone much like yourself," sighed Traru. "She wants to sail, to be a silnik."

"And what is wrong with that?" asked Maru.

"The sea will not be kind."

"The sea or those who sail upon her?" shot back Maru a little more intensely than she intended. "Sorry, Uncle. If a woman can call the dolfers, then she should be good enough to be a silnik or a captain as any man."

"First you will have to convince The Silnik of that, niece, since he has ruled against women sailing. And with good reason as there is a base rabble that only respects physical power."

"The pirates."

"The pirates," agreed the older man.

"I need to learn to sail," said Maru.

The older man turned in her direction as if he watched her. "Why, Maru?"

"I must, otherwise I am useless."

"Never useless, Maru."

"No mate and no prospects of one, then what am I good for? I am not needed for anything but decoration."

"Do not lower your value," said her uncle, "If you really intend to be a captain that is something you need to learn. Always sell yourself as something valuable and others will see you that way."

"All people seem to see in me is The Silnik's daughter."

"True, and it comes with benefits and some liabilities, but Maru is more."

"I have to sail," she said softly but firmly.

Her uncle leaned towards her. "Why, Maru?"

"Today I was on the outlook with the twins, and I saw shadows on the water coming from the west and for a moment I thought they were the shadows of enormous birds. When I looked again they were merely shadows."

"One often sees shapes in the clouds, Maru," said the older man reassuringly.

"I have to battle those shadows, Uncle," said Maru softly.

"It need not be you, Maru."

Maru closed her eyes, "No, I think it has to be me and I have to know enough to sail. I have to be a sailor."

"Maru, if something should happen to you, your father would be devastated."

"And what will happen if I don't?" she asked the man.

"Are you so certain?"

"Yes."

"Do I hear the bell for dinner?" the man asked taking her arm.

"Will you support my request when I approach my father?"

"The Silnik will do as he deems necessary," said Traru ambiguously.

* * *

CHAPTER 3

Maru did not have the opportunity the night before to speak with her father. So, this morning, she decided to see him before he began his official day. She would not be allowed to interrupt him once he started seeing citizens and their issues. She was hoping to catch him at his breakfast, a time he was often alone or only with an aide.

She rehearsed her words again as she hurried down the hall in a simple cotton sarong. She opened her mouth in preparation as she stepped into the room. She came to a sudden stop as she realized her father was not alone. Sitting next to him was her uncle and a little behind him stood her cousin.

Her father looked up in surprise. "Well, Maru, you're up early."

"I wished a word with you father." Maru looked at the various faces.

"Perhaps another time today, sea foam," said her father gently.

"Has my uncle told you what I wish to discuss?"

Mertin looked at the man next to him. "No, we have been talking of other things."

"Silnik, let Tranin and me give Maru her audience with you. Our business can wait. We shall be in the hall." Traru had risen and his son had him by his elbow to guide him to the door.

The Silnik indicated a seat. Maru decided to stand, so she shook her head. Her father's face looked more lined than she remembered, and his blonde hair showed more than a few streaks that were white. His white was not due to the bleaching of the sun.

He smiled at her and Maru drew a breath.

"I want to learn to sail," she got it out as quickly as she could.

He frowned. He studied her and started to respond.

Maru quickly cut his response off, "I know Uncle Traru could not find me a suitable mate and maybe never will. I need to be useful. I need to be a sailor."

"No. No, woman may sail. I forbid it." He was frowning.

"That makes no sense, Father. A woman may be just as good as a man."

"Maru, sailing is not the same as the jaunts we have taken as a family."

"Father, I must." Maru looked around briefly around the room. "If you will not allow my plan then I will..."

"Maru, do not make rash vows. It is too dangerous."

"I would be safe enough with Traru and Tranin."

"Maru, you are my daughter and the risk of something happening to you is too great."

"You mean the pirates."

"Yes, the pirates. They are not some romantic or over exaggerated threat. What they have done with people, with women is evil. What they would do with The Silnik's daughter does not bear thinking about. We will not discuss this further. There will be a mate for you Maru. I can feel it. Have patience."

Maru nodded her head but could not feel his confidence.

He stood and went to his daughter. He pulled her to his chest and hugged her tight. "I lost your mother early. I do not wish to lose you also." His grip was firm, and she could hear emotions in his voice that he did not usually share with her. "Patience, Minnow."

Maru nodded and turned her head away as she left the room, so he would not see her tears. She ran into her uncle.

"Not the answer you wanted?" he asked softly.

"Not the answer I need," she replied.

"Are you certain?" he asked.

She nodded trying to keep the pictures of the cloud shadows that raced over Grantoli from her mind.

"Tranin and I leave tomorrow. Early."

Maru looked up at her uncle and realized that she was alone with him. Tranin was nowhere in view.

"I would not take aboard my vessel anyone who cannot figure a way to get onto it unseen. Sailors have always had to be resourceful."

* * *

CHAPTER 4

Maru waited below. She knew when Traru and Tranin came on board as they were arguing.

"We cannot take this boat out with just me to sail her."

"You can manage."

"Father," the exasperation in Tranin's voice was clear.

"Then go and get Welden and Parder. They'll be at *The Silly Goose*."

"It takes at least four. I'll find Bardt."

"No. Only Welden, Parder and you."

"Why not Bardt?"

"His wife just had a baby; he is needed here."

"Fine, I'll get someone else."

"No," said his father.

There was a pause. "What are you up to silnik?"

"Something that needs to have as few tongues as possible and ones that know how to be held."

"The Silnik gave you a job?"

"Not exactly. Get the others and get back here. I want to catch the tide."

Tranin stormed off the ship judging by the noise his footfalls made.

Maru remained where she was. The hatch cover opened to reveal a dark head against a star filled sky.

"Well, you managed to elude the harbor watch. Nice job, Minnow."

"How did you know I was here, then?" asked Maru.

"The Laughing Dolfer hasn't smelled of jasmine perfume since my mate died. How are you dressed?"

"Cotton kilt and top."

"Shoes?"

"None, should I have worn them?"

"Useless on board. How long is your hair and what have you done with it?"

"Middle of my back. I braided it."

He grunted. "It'll do. We may have to cut the hair."

Maru moved towards the hatch.

"No," said the man, "Say hidden until we are well to sea. My son will not be understanding. Spend the time recalling any knots I taught you as a child."

Maru moved back into the corner. "Thank you, Uncle."

The man turned his head as if looking at her. "Do not thank me yet, Minnow. This may not end the way you wish it." He dropped the lid back in place

Maru curled into a small ball and felt the ship sway and creak slightly on the harbor waves.

Tranin returned quickly with two extra footfalls. "We're back."

"I could tell. You move like a seal on land," complained his father. "I could have heard you in my sleep."

"I can still get Bardt."

"Cast off," said Traru. "I want to be past the patrol ships and out of sight of Grantoli before sun up."

Maru could hear men moving forward and aft clearing lines. The ship seemed to bob free of its confinement to the dock.

"Father, what are we up to?" Tranin's voice was set low but as they were almost directly outside the porthole nearest her she could hear him clearly.

Traru did not answer.

Tranin's voice carried an edge that she did not normally associate with her cousin. "You know I can dream a little. Whatever you are planning is...precarious."

Traru did not respond.

"Can you not even tell me?"

"When the time is right," said Traru finally. "And then I am counting on you..."

"Dolfers," cried another voice. Maru thought it might be Parder, although it had been a while since she had heard his voice.

"Well," said her uncle brighter, "There's a good omen."

Maru remained where she was, listening to the sounds of the ship and its crew as they crossed the harbor and then exchanged shouted greetings to the guard towers at the harbor entrance. She knew when they had moved into the open ocean, clear of the land's protection as the ship danced more briskly. Then the breeze really caught their sails and the vessel's motion smoothed out into a glide.

Greetings and names were given as they later crossed the perimeter of the guard ships. The Trawn appellation gave them ready passage without the suggestion of being boarded or searched.

As the sky paled to morning gold she heard her uncle say, "Tranin, go and get an extra line."

"This one is enough."

"I want a newer one. There should be one below."

"If you weren't my father, I'd say you were getting cantankerous, silnik."

"Just do as you're told. In fact, that's the best advice I can give you for this entire trip."

The hatch was opened, and a pair of legs descended the ladder accompanied by grumbling. Hunched over because of the space, Tranin turned. In his surprise he started to straighten bumping his head on the ceiling of the space. "Minnow!"

"Hello, Tranin."

He looked up at the hatch then back at her. "I see the secrecy. The Silnik agreed to let you sail," he said with a smile.

"Well..., a silnik agreed."

Tranin's smile disappeared. "You don't have your father's permission?"

"Tranin, I had to do this. Your father understood. Mine did not."

Tranin was halfway up the ladder when Maru grabbed his kilt to stop him.

He looked back at her. "Nothing good will come of this," he said. "We have to turn back."

"No," she said fiercely. "No, I must sail."

"I cannot be a party to this, Maru." He brushed off her hand and continued up the steps.

Maru hurried up the ladder after him. Tranin was already confronting Traru who was seated near the ship's wheel.

"You knew she was here!" he accused the man. Tranin looked at the man at the helm and another who was tidying lines. "And these two? Was I the last to know?"

The man at the helm stared at Maru then to Tranin and then his silnik. "Silnik?"

"They didn't know any more than I have told you, Tranin. Parder," shouted Traru, "Leave the lines and come aft. Minnow, you too."

Maru tried not to trip as she moved towards Traru's position. The sailor at the helm, Welden, tried to keep his eyes on the horizon, but they kept darting back to Maru.

The world still hung in that balance where the stars' rule was quietly being supplanted by a brightening sky. More than the equilibrium between night and day was being decided.   She was facing aft and could see only open sea. They were well clear of any eyes on Grantoli mount. At this moment only these four men knew where she was and would decide what her future would be.

Parder grunted as he came to fill in a space next to Tranin.

"You all remember The Minnow, Maru?"

The two men nodded and looked cautiously at Tranin whose face was angry.

"She's going to be our fourth pair of hands."

"Silnik Traru," began Tranin formally, "we cannot ship The Silnik's daughter with us, without his permission. Do you have that permission?"

Parder's eyes wandered from father to son with an occasional stop at Maru. Welden stared determinedly at the horizon.

"No," said Traru.

"Then you have just kidnapped The Silnik's daughter and made us all pirates."

"You are only pirates," inserted Maru quickly, "If you have taken me against my will."

"Your will is not important here," said Tranin ignoring her as he stared at his father.

"My will is the only thing important here," said Maru stepping forward. The man's eyes turned towards her. "I blackmailed your father and if anyone is here against their will, it is the four of you."

"You blackmailed my father?" said Tranin with a smirk.

"Ask him if he wanted to do this," demanded Maru.

"Well, silnik?" asked his son. "Are you aiding and abetting this one willingly?"

"Tranin," began the man then paused. "No, I don't want her here anymore than you do."

"And just how did she blackmail you?" he persisted.

"I would not exactly call it blackmail," said the older man. "Let us say, I was persuaded against my better judgment."

Tranin looked at Maru. "The Silnik will not see it that way."

"Then we best not get caught until Maru gets what she wants," said the older man.

"And what do you want, Maru, other than to see the four of us hang from the gallows or rotting in a prison."

Maru glared at him. "No blame shall fall on you. This was my idea and my father will certainly be willing to believe I instigated the whole trip."

"What do *we* have to do, Maru? What are your demands to release *my* father from your hold?" Tranin was angry in a manner Maru had not seen before.

"He promised to teach me to sail." She held her chin up.

Welden's and Parder's faces relaxed some.

"She was always quick to learn. It should take less than a month," said Traru. "We'll keep our course southerly and use the Far Isles for a start. Maru, show Tranin where that extra line can be found."

Tranin gave his father a black look before he marched back to the hatch. Maru looked at the older man who nodded in her direction then she quickly followed her cousin below into the still dark cabin.

He turned on her the moment she stepped off the last rung. "How dare you do this to my father? Just because you are The Silnik's daughter does not mean you may have everything you want."

"What do you know of my getting everything I want," she spat back at him. "You sail where you wish; you go where you want. No one stops you from feeling the breeze on your face, from being useful."

Tranin stepped back at the intensity of her rebuttal. "You're a woman and The Silnik's daughter. You cannot do the things I do. You are not a man."

"Why?" she asked.

"Why?" he repeated in confusion. "I just told you. You are a woman, and Silnik Mertin's daughter."

"Why should I not sail?" she demanded again. "I can pull my weight. I can read some stars, enough to locate the compass directions. Why should I be confined to perfumed halls and tedious conversations?"

"Maru, we'll find you a silnik and then you can raise your own family..."

"That may not be enough, Tranin, don't you see?" She felt the comforting rock of the ship beneath her bare feet. "There is a restlessness in me that cannot sit and wait."

"This is madness," he said throwing up his arms.

"No," she said softly, calmly, "Madness is what would have come upon me if I had remained in Grantoli."

Tranin's eyes looked troubled. "Maru, let us turn back."

She returned his regard. "I cannot, Tranin."

* * *

CHAPTER 5

Maru finished her splice. She double checked it before she gathered up the line to take to Traru. Her hands were calloused, her skin bronzed and her hair bleached almost white. Welden had the wheel. Parder was keeping watch and Tranin was arguing with his father. She didn't need to guess what the topic was. As the month had progressed Tranin had become terser in his conversations with her and the last two days had avoided her completely which was a good trick considering the size of the ship.

The younger man saw the direction she was headed and for once stood his ground.

"Silnik, the line you requested," said Maru setting the test in the older man's hands under the glare of her cousin.

She watched as Traru ran his hands over the join she had made. He frowned in concentration as he traced each strand from one rope to the other. Finally, he nodded and tossed the line at his son. "Good. Well, Sailor Minnow, time's up. You've had your month."

"Yes, silnik," she replied with a heavy heart.

"Tranin, take the wheel." Tranin looked as if he would counter his father's order. "Set a course for Grantoli."

"No," spoke Maru quickly. "One last thing Silniks Traru and Tranin, Sailors Welden and Parder."

Tranin frowned at the formal naming.

"Yes, Maru?" asked her uncle politely.

"I wish to be Tested," she said with as much courage as she could find. This was an uncertain move. Would they come?

Her uncle stood deep in thought. Her cousin and the two sailors looked stunned.

"She can't," stammered Tranin. "You can't let her. It is bad enough that we gave way to her wish to sail. If we lose her to the sea, there will be no excuse to give The Silnik." The other two men moved restlessly. Parder nodded and frowned.

"It is my right to ask for the Test," said Maru. "Do you deny a sailor the right?" she questioned Tranin but included the other two men in her question.

"Father, no. She cannot do this, she will drown."

"Will she?" asked his father. "Her mother didn't."

Maru opened her mouth in surprise. Her mother had swum the Test? Had been a silnik? She could see even Tranin had not known either.

Traru straightened and looked at Maru with milky eyes. "Sailor Maru of the Clan Myrten, Daughter of The Southern Silnik Mertin, you wish to be Tested?"

Maru felt a chill. Both her parents calling the dolfers was no guarantee that she could. She looked only at her uncle. "I do, Silnik Traru."

Tranin went to interject but his father's words drowned out his response. "Then I declare to all that Sailor Maru at her own request shall be Tested. Parder, Tranin, drop the sails. This spot is as good as another."

"If she fails, you will have killed The Silnik's daughter," hissed Tranin, almost spitting as he spoke.

"If she fails, my niece dies. Do you imagine I care what The Silnik thinks after that?" replied his father. "See to the sails."

The younger man looked down at the spliced line in his hands and changed his mind. He bumped Maru hard in his passing, thrusting the line she had spliced into her hands.

"Relax and do not fight the water, Minnow. If it will not be your second mother, she will not listen to you." Maru looked to her uncle. He nodded as she did not interrupt him. "Do you know what the dolfer voices sound like?"

"No, uncle."

He sighed. "Well perhaps this was ill-conceived. You may still step back from the edge."

"I asked," she said.

He nodded, "When you are in the water, listen. You will either hear them or you will not. There is nothing more we can do for you."

"Thank you for believing in me, Uncle," she rose up and kissed him on his cheek.

She pulled off her top and unfastened the kilt. The ship bobbed slightly in the open sea. The summer weather had been cooling over the last week and now the clouds were growing thicker.

"Very well, sailor. Let the Test begin."

Maru dove off the side of the boat before Tranin could change his mind and decide to stop her. She surfaced a little way from the vessel.

"That is far enough, Maru," cried out her uncle.

Maru smiled and waved at the figures on the boat. If she failed, she could be right beside the boat and it would not matter. If one wanted the Test they succeeded or drowned. No middle ground existed, even for The Silnik's daughter.

Relax, her uncle had said. She was tense, she realized. The water was still warm this far south. She lay back, closed her eyes and listened. Canvas sail and line slapped and jangled against the masts and spars. Water splashed against the side of the ship. Listen, he had said.

She could hear her heart pounding in her chest and her gulps as she took in air. Relax and listen.

She swayed in the slight swells. It was soothing. If the sun had been out her face would have felt warm and she would have been very comfortable. Listen, she reminded herself. What would the dolfers sound like? They made a chittery noise when they wanted to talk to you in the harbor, but she was pretty sure that was not what she should be listening for, or was it?

The dolfers, she thought of their blue-gray sleek forms that cut the water as birds cleaved the air. They could easily out race any craft. They seemed to delight in riding the bow waves and swimming circles around ships. Although they were creatures of the water, they still came to surface for air as did land animals, so they were not fish, but brothers that had somehow managed to return more fully to the sea.

'Where are you?' she called out in her mind. 'Do you know me? Will you come to me?'

For the first time entering the water Maru shivered. Had she been arrogant? Did she presume to something she was not capable or deserving of? Had she just condemned the men on the boat to her father's anger when they lay her lifeless body at his feet? Her mother had been a silnik, she thought fiercely. A woman could be a silnik.

She shivered again, and the water felt not so warm. She felt various muscles start to tense and cramp.

Relax, she commanded her body. Her mind began to run in all directions with fear. Relax, she thought softly. Relax and listen. If she failed, she failed. Her father had to understand. He knew her nature. She had to try. She felt another muscle in her leg cramp.

Relax. I am part of the sea, living or dying or dead. Somewhere she could hear arguing. Relax. She was rocking in the waves. Yes, they were cold, but that did not matter.

She opened her eyes in surprise as water washed over her face. She sputtered to the surface. The wind had picked up and the waves were rougher. She looked around for *The Laughing Dolfer*. She and the ship had drifted quite a way apart and the fact she could hear arguing meant that the people involved had to be shouting.

For the first time she really considered the fact that she might...just...fail the Test. Another muscle cramped in the cold. Oh Father, she thought, I am sorry. She wasn't sure if it was a tear or just a drop of salt water that slid across her face.

The dolfers weren't coming. Perhaps she had been too proud. Perhaps Tranin was right to be angry at her. She had just condemned decent men to whatever judgment her father dealt them. 'Farewell,' she thought. 'I am sorry.' She raised an arm to wave at the men on the ship. She wasn't certain if they even saw the action as she slid down into the trough of the next wave and dipped beneath the water. Soon, they would not know where she was. 'At least let them bring my body home,' thought Maru to the universe in general.

Someone laughed at her.

'Let them have the body in their mourning.' The sky and water were a matching gray. Maru didn't bob so lightly on the water. She managed to keep her lips above the waterline, but it was an effort, one that was quickly tiring her. "Do not be cruel,' she whispered in her head. 'You have my spirit, it is gone. Let them have the body.'

Something thumped her soundly in her stomach, causing her to lose that last breath she had been holding, but also propelling her clear of the choppy waves. She gasped deeply before she fell back into the water, this time face downward.

A shadow came out of the dark depths, stream line like a shark. It rammed her, pushing her upwards. She grasped at the shape hoping to keep it at arms distance. Her hands slide over a smooth surface with a jelly like give. This was not mahew skin.

'Hold on, on, on,' came a thought into her mind as her head cleared the waves. She grasped for a hold and found a firm projection. The animal pulled her forward. Maru clung with both hands to her hold of the animal's dorsal fin. She tried not to cough but take measured breaths. She was cold, and her hands started to lose their grip.

"There! There she is!" She heard a boat dropped into the water and the creak of oars in locks as men grunted in effort.

The animal was no longer pulling her forward but gently buoyed her slack body up.

"How many?" asked a voice from a distance as hands pulled her from the water.

"Nineteen, twenty," muttered a voice still counting.

A thick woolen blanket was wrapped around her and someone held her tightly.

"I'm sorry, Tranin," she said shivering in his hold.

"Hush, silnik," he said. "I apologize for doubting you." He pinned the blanket closed at a shoulder.

She opened her eyes. "But you are right to be angry."

"We'll discuss that another day." He set her in the bottom of the boat and found his place at a set of oars. Welden pulled on another pair, grinning from ear to ear. "Twenty-five, Silnik Maru!"

By the time they reached The Laughing Dolfer, Maru attempted to climb to the little vessel. Thank goodness Tranin helped her. On board Traru sent her below to warm up and dress. Someone had lit a brazier that warmed the cabin. The clothes she had discarded earlier where laid out neatly. Her fingers numbly tied the kilt and pulled the cotton shirt over her torso. She pushed the stray strands of hair that had worked free of her braid away from her face. She took a slow deep breath and willed some strength back into her legs.

On deck, the men stood waiting as she exited the hatch. Traru and his son stood at the center each wearing a silnik's red sash of command. Her uncle held another red sash. Maru went to stand in front of him reflecting how narrowly she came to be able to stand here. She did not feel jubilant. She did not feel victorious. She felt rather small, extremely lucky and very owing.

Off the side of the boat she spotted the dolfers. One of them rose up above the water on his back tail and chittered at her loudly. Yes, she was properly chastised. She hung her head at her hubris.

"Witnesses!" cried Traru's voice loudly enough to have been heard the length of a warship, "What are the findings!"

"Five and Twenty Dolfers," declared Welden.

"Twenty and Five," cried Parder.

"And you will so swear to all men?"

"To all, men or women," answered Parder.

"Aye," agreed Welden adding, "And Intare freeze us if we lie."

"Well then, Sailor Maru, no more, but Silnik Maru this day. Wear the color of command with wisdom and discernment." He reached around her and tied a red sash at her waist.

"Thank you," she said bowing to the witnesses and then to the silniks and finally she turned towards the dolfer who still eyed her from the water. "And to my brothers and sisters of the sea."

The dolfer sank quickly into the waves. She was reminded again, that she should be chastised for thinking it a game. At that moment all twenty-five animals broke the surface of the water simultaneously, arcing higher than her head to dive once again into the water. The wind caught the spray they created and blew it onto Maru who had taken a step back at the spectacle.

One last dolfer surface quietly next to the boat. Maru looked to the men who waited.

Maru leaned over the railing. 'Thank you,' she thought as clearly as she could, 'for sparing my father grief, for sparing these men an ignoble end.'

The dolfer looked at her with its dark eye then flipped his head back as if agreeing and then spun on its tail, turned and dove, slapping the water with his tail. The splash coated the girl in spray.

Arms pulled her back from the rail. Tranin stood at the wheel. Welden let her go and headed to the lines of the slack sheets. Parder was already raising sail.

Traru caught Maru's elbow and headed for the bow of the ship. "Well, you did not let your father's, or mother's, clans down, Minnow."

"I'm sorry, Uncle. I did not consider that I might fail. It would have gone badly for the four of you." Maru considered how close it had been. "Tranin was right to be angry with me."

"He will be unhappy with you for quite a while, Maru, but even so he will do his duty to you as The Silnik's daughter, but more importantly as family."

Maru shivered and looked up to find the sky had clouded over. "I did not mean to make him my enemy."

"No, he is not your enemy. He is just angry in his concern. You can navigate, sail and are recognized as a silnik. You know what I know, but have not the experience, Minnow. Experience counts for a lot with the sea. Experience and your heart. Your heart, so like your mother's, will compensate for your lack of experience...I think."

"Father will not let me loose, so it will hardly matter, uncle."

"Oh, I think it will."

"You see a future?"

"I see many futures," smiled the old man sadly, "I just don't know which one will become reality. The Test is more than calling the dolfers, Maru. It defines the person."

"Jazmin," clarified Maru, "said she did not understand how the dolfers can answer the call of pirates."

"What do you think now?"

"I do not know. I certainly was not worth the saving."

"To your family, of course you are. And, in some way they judge."

"It is time for me to go home and carry out my role," said Maru standing a little straighter. "Not what I want, but what is needed."

The old man rested his warm hand on her head. "You will always be able to do what is needed, Maru."

She felt an almost physical touch envelope her completely. She blinked.

Her uncle bent double and then did something she had never seen him do. He was violently seasick.

"Tranin!" she screamed as she caught at the older man as he collapsed. She got one of his arms over her shoulder to keep him from falling to the deck.

CHAPTER 6

"What the Intare did you do to him, Maru?" shouted Tranin as he lifted his father out of her hold.

Maru sprang ahead to get the hatch open and climbed down so she could catch her uncle's form as Tranin passed him to her.

"Nothing," she said trying to figure out what had just happened. She helped stretch her uncle on the berth and found a blanket to cover him with. His face was ashy, but his pulse seemed strong. Tranin pushed her aside to check the pulse himself.

"You know how badly your father would have treated him, Maru, if the dolfers had not showed up. And that would have been nothing compared to how he would have felt about himself."

"Yes, Tranin, I already apologized to Traru. I am sorry." She felt tears.

"Well, I suppose you will say it turned out well," he said gruffly.

Maru shook her head. "I don't know. I'm not dead but..." at that moment a cold blast of air found its way into the cabin through the open hatch as the boat lurched.

Tranin eyed her and the building storm outside. "Let us get you to Grantoli. You *can* keep out of trouble until then?"

The man headed for the ladder. "Holler if you need me." He dropped the hatch with a thud.

Maru added two coals to the brazier and set it closer to the berth her uncle rested in. She found the kettle full of water and set it on the fire to boil.

His color was better, and his breathing seemed normal. Perhaps he just slept now, she thought, and moved to a spot where she could keep an eye on him.

"Is he gone?"

"Are you faking, Uncle?" she asked in asperity.

"Not entirely," he sighed. "It has been such a long time that it took me so completely by surprise."

"What?" asked Maru, moving close and checking that the man was covered.

"Blessing you," he sighed.

"You blessed me?" she asked in surprise.

"It may have been a curse," he said opening his eyes as he thought about it. "They are much one and the same thing and I hadn't intended to do either."

"Well, you frightened us."

"Was I sick?" he asked.

"All over the deck. I think that is what alarmed us the most."

"Good," nodded Traru with a smile.

"Good?" exclaimed Maru.

"All real blessings are followed by physical depletion of the body, either fainting or vomiting."

Maru shivered. "Why did you do it?"

"I had not intended to, Minnow. Sometimes the dream takes you where it will."

Maru sat with him quietly until the water started to boil. She fixed him a cup of tea adding plenty of sugar to combat the cold and give him energy. "Here, drink this," she said handing him the cup. He sat up and drank slowly.

"Why did you let me sail with you?"

He sighed. "You had trouble making others take your worries about the shadows seriously. Oh yes, they worry about the pirates, everyone worries about the pirates, but your worries are of a different nature. And no one was listening, not even your father. Not because he thought you lied, Maru, but because pursuing your dream was dangerous and had no clear future. Do you see one?" he asked her.

She shook her head, then said, "No," very softly, "only the shadows."

"Well because you are so like your mother, I believed you. If your dreams said you must be a sailor, then you must. But you didn't tell me your dreams said you had to be a silnik." He chuckled softly.

"I am sorry again, Uncle. I didn't think that one through, it came out of my mouth before I considered it." Maru felt she would be expressing regret to him for a long time.

"Don't apologize, Maru."

"I have seen my pride today, Uncle. It was not pretty."

He patted her hand. "Give me another cup of tea. You should drink one yourself."

"Why does no one speak of my mother being a silnik?" she asked refilling his cup.

"She went down with her ship. The dolfers brought her body to Grantoli, to your father. She was given honors and returned to the sea. Your father was not The Silnik then, but he took it brutally. Blamed himself. A storm can take anyone, there was no blame, but he did because he gave into her desire to sail."

"Why should a woman not sail?" she asked.

"Why not," agreed her uncle. "Most women are more sensible then men and better at bargaining on merchandise." He sighed, "But the pirates are no respecters of either sex and after losing your mother, when your father did become The Silnik of the Southern Clans he ordered all women from the decks. I did not agree. A woman, or man, of spirit should be allowed to make their own decisions, but Tara's death shook him deeply."

"So, you took a chance when you agreed to let me sail," said Maru realizing that Tranin perhaps had been right to say she had gotten her way.

"I could only honor my sister by giving you your chance, Maru," said the man softly. "She would have been very proud of her daughter, that I know. What the Silnik says, we will find out."

Maru took the empty tea cup as the older man lay back in the berth. In moments she could tell he slept. Maru pondered all the things that had occurred and worried at what was yet to come.

She was still worrying at the future when she went to spell Welden on deck. Not hers specifically, but Grantoli's in general.

She kept a hand on a line as the water washed the deck. The day had not lightened, and it was hard to tell when night really came. The waters were deep to the south, so they sailed without worry about grounding. Eventually they would determine exactly where they were, until then they would face into the storm and ride it out.

She and the men took turns going below to warm up and catch some sleep. They had to drag Tranin from the wheel. Welden twisted the man's arm behind his back and walked him to the hatch. "Get some rest, Silnik Tranin or we'll replace you with your cousin." Maru had seen the brief black look he had given her before another sheet of rain cut the view.

Maru took her turn at the wheel and held on for dear life. Although wire-y from the month at sea, she wasn't as massive as the men and had to fight the ship with everything she had. She suspected Tranin came back early to take back over. She thanked him as she relinquished the helm and found lines to check. Her pride had put them all in danger enough in one day.

About mid-night the wind dropped, and the clouds opened up. They all gave a collective sigh of relief. Judging by the stars, they had made very good time with the storm's help. They turned east. Tomorrow they could be in Grantoli. At the thought Maru almost wept a second time in that day.

Traru joined them on deck and they ate a simple meal in the quiet air surround by the still rough seas.

About the third hour after the middle of the night the fog rolled in.

* * *

CHAPTER 7

"We're too far west," said Parder again.

Tranin agreed, again.

They were using the stars directly above to guide them as they could see nothing at the ocean's level.

"Head east," said Traru. "We aren't far enough north to run into shoals and we certainly don't want to be sailing here when the fog lifts. The currents should help carry us."

Maru kept silent. Her experience counted for nothing as she saw it and she was the ultimate reason they were here.

The sky was lightening to the east as they sailed. The night stars didn't quite match the dawning hour, thought Maru, wondering if she had missed something in one of the lessons. Tranin seemed to keep checking the sky frequently too.

"Silnik," began Tranin.

"Hush," said Traru as he turned in the direction they sailed. "Do you smell it?"

The others looked at each other and sniffed the wind.

"Smoke," said Traru, "and something else."

Smoke was good, thought Maru, smiling. It would be the kitchen fires of Grantoli.

"I don't smell it, yet," replied Tranin, "But if you do we cannot be far from the harbor entrance."

Traru shook his head. "No, you should not smell it this far away."

"Sail!" shouted Parder who was forward as lookout.

"Down the hatch," ordered Traru grabbing a surprised Maru and pulling her towards the cabin opening. "Get the sash off and hide it and your knife. You know the panel. And keep quiet."

The men looked as surprised as Maru as she hustled below.

"Pirates," she heard Traru say as she locked the hatch from within.

They were too close to Grantoli for pirates. Maybe Traru was being cautious this near to home.

"Can we out run the ship?" she heard one of the men ask.

"If it was one, I would give us excellent odds. Do you see more?" asked Traru.

"Two on the port," said a soft voice she recognized as Tranin's.

"Another one starboard and one due ahead."

"Intare, we must have just sailed into the middle of them. Don't they see us?" asked Tranin.

"I hope not," said Traru. "Perhaps we are too small, and they are not expecting to see anyone. Get down. Play dead. Perhaps they will think us abandoned and not worth their effort to stop."

She could hear nothing but the creak of the ships that surrounded their small vessel. Had the others set no watch or lookout? How could they avoid seeing them?

Now Maru could faintly smell smoke.

"Intare," whispered one of the men on deck.

Through the port hole she could see the fog glowing. It resolved to be a ship low in the water, burning. Another ship slid past blocking her view. She pulled back to the side, not that anyone from another ship would see her if they hadn't already seen their vessel or if they saw it they thought it occupied by the dead.

"Ship!" came a cry to the port. There was a murmuring of voices.

"Get a grapple on it," shouted a voice.

Maru's heart sank. She could hear the hook the pirates cast land soundly above her. Five were too few against warships.

There was the chunk of an axe and Tranin shouting. "Quickly, underway."

The little ship came to life and the wind briefly seemed their ally, but arrows rained down and she heard someone cry out, Parder she thought, and a splash as he hit the water.

She heard feet land on the craft and it rocked under more men as they joined the first. Then all was calm.

One last pair of feet landed heavily on the ship causing it to shift in the water.

"What have we here? Who are you and what port?"

"Fishermen, Grantoli," replied Traru softly.

"Fishermen. Where are your nets?"

"Stored against the storm," answered Traru reasonably.

"Where are your fish?"

"You expect anyone to catch fish in the storm?" asked Traru with a laugh.

"I don't like you old man."

Traru wisely kept silent.

"Who else is on board?"

"Just our fishing party."

"Open the hatch." The voice seemed to be speaking to another man.

"Yes, captain."

Maru drew back as far as she could into hiding, but there was little left for this ploy. She changed her mind and stood clearly at the foot of the ladder. The hatch was tried then an axe brought down on it. The wood shattered. A man thrust a torch in her direction and seeing her gave a cry.

He was shoved aside by another whose head was a black silhouette against the burning fog. "A girl. You would take fright at your own shadow. You, get up here!"

Maru climbed the ladder and stepped on the deck. The face was still in shadows as he looked at her and turned to Traru. "Who is she?" The profile of the man was sharp.

"My daughter. Minnow, go stand next to your brother."

Maru did not need to be told twice. She was not as tall as Tranin, but their features clearly defined them as related.

The voice looked at her again, this time noting more than her face. She looked at Tranin, who appeared to have a bruised cheek but otherwise seemed unharmed. "A handsome pair," he said, looking at her again. "Yes, we'll keep these two. The rest," he gave a jerk to his head.

Maru went to cry out, but Tranin caught her hand and squeezed it tightly. Welden, gave his captor a fist to the face before he dove overboard. Maru could not see where he surfaced if he did. Traru, backed up and tripped as an arrow planted itself in the mast near where he had been standing. He fell backwards into the dark water. Men raced to the side to search for the two men and not a few arrows were shot into the sea, but with the questionable light, Maru thought they did not hit anything.

"Well the sea can claim them," said the voice with a laugh, "but she did leave me the prizes." He looked at Tranin. "You will clean up well enough. Don't know how long you will last at hard labor, but longer than most I wager. And little sister," the man smiled, "Yes, you are a money maker. And just when I thought we had cleaned everything of value out of Grantoli." He smiled. "Take them on board *The Raven*."

As she was pulled away Maru watched as the man walked around *The Laughing Dolfer* and smiled at his prize. She was separated from Tranin, but she watched him as he signed the clan word for patience before they were separated below.

The room she was cast into held a dozen women already. She made it an unlucky thirteen. She smiled internally for a second, unlucky for the pirate. She looked around as the door closed with a solid ring behind her.

"Who are you?" she asked the group.

A woman handed a trembling woman into another's care before coming forward. "We should be asking you."

"Sailor folk from the east," lied Maru thinking of how much value she should give herself. She was certain her uncle would advise her to down play her worth in this situation. "We came to visit Grantoli, to see family."

"What family?" demanded the woman suspiciously.

Maru was stuck. "Traru is a relation of my mother," she said.

The woman studied her slowly then nodded, "You look like the Trawn. Well, your cousin was not in port when the pirates came, so perhaps you will see him again someday." She gave a mirthless smile.

Maru remembered Traru's blank gaze as he went over the side of the ship. It was not likely.

"And your name, daughter of the Trawn?"

"They call me Minnow."

"Not very pretty," the woman said with a sigh, "But I suppose that hardly matters."

"How, how did this happen?"

"You mean the raid?" The woman had crossed back to wrap an arm around the woman she had been sheltering when Maru had been cast into the room. "They came a day ago just in front of the storm."

"Grantoli, is known for its defenses," puzzled Maru.

"Grantoli has been upside down for a month, Minnow. Ever since The Silnik suddenly sent all available warships off in every compass direction. Then two days ago most of the rest of the fleet took chase after a pirate armada that sailed around the peninsula headed east. Those ships had not returned when this second fleet of pirates sailed through the guard towers. There were too few left to stop them." She gently stroked the hair of the woman she was holding. "No one left," she sighed.

"What about the Silnik and his family," asked Maru.

"We're pretty sure he is still safely behind his walls with those citizens they could get in, but other than the occasional arrow, they were outnumbered. At least they can bury the dead."

"He'll do something," said Maru fiercely.

The woman looked at her, passed the woman she was holding to another again and took Maru by the arm. "Minnow, The Silnik will do what he can, but not for us. We're among the dead now. How old are you?"

"Twenty summers."

"Tell them fourteen, you might pass. Virgin?"

"Yes."

"Tell the one in charge."

"What?"

"That or he'll rape you now. He was working his way through us when they stopped for your vessel."

"Won't they rape me anyway?"

"You're worth more as a virgin. If nothing else, it will give you time. Perhaps you can even find a knife before the moment comes." The woman looked around her as if she could find one in the cell they occupied. "They don't value us much, but virginity is a commodity in demand and it doesn't last."

The door opened with a bang making the women nearest jump back, crowding Maru to the wall.

"Send the last girl brought to the cell to the door," boomed a voice.

Maru worked her way towards the door as the women drew back to make room for her. Her advisor stepped between Maru and the man.

"Leave the child alone."

"She's no child," sneered the man.

"She's a virgin, that makes her a child," said the woman firmly.

"Get out of my way," he said backhanding her. Maru caught her and gently passed her back and out of the way.

"Are you a virgin?" the man demanded.

Maru found it impossible to speak confronted with the face so close and the mood so ugly. She nodded.

"Show me," he demanded.

Maru stripped off her kilt and spread her legs. She felt the man's fingers test her words.

He stared at her then shook his head in anger as he walked away. He turned at the door and pointed at the woman he had hit. "You!" He gestured with his hand that she should follow.

Maru stepped between the woman and the door. "No."

"Get out of her way," said the man with a snarl, "or when your time comes, you will regret it."

The woman pushed Maru aside and stepped after the man with her head held high.

"What is her name?" whispered Maru realizing she did not know her benefactress.

"Darlow," whispered another.

"I will pray for the sea to be kind to Darlow and curse her enemies," said Maru feeling a rage build and grip her to the point she could not move or see. She fell to floor sick and then senseless.

When she came to, Darlow was pushing the fine strands of hair away from her face.

"Are you okay?" asked Maru.

"As much as can be expected," said the woman. "They said you cursed my enemies."

"Do not be disappointed if I cannot make it come true," said Maru softly.

Darlow smiled. "No one ever cursed my enemies for me before. It is enough. Are you okay now?"

"Yes. Tend to the needier," requested Maru as she pondered the future.

* * *

CHAPTER 8

His name was Lorland, Maru learned. Merely, Captain Lorland. She was glad he was not a silnik. Like her step-mother, she found it hard to stomach the idea that the dolfers might have picked him, or any pirate, for a silnik.

He went through the women almost daily. To keep them fresh, he said. Each time he had hungry eyes for Maru but did nothing more.

They were not the only women captured from Grantoli, but Lorland had taken these, the ones he deemed the best, for himself. They were, or rather had been, lovely women. Life in a holding cell on a rolling ship and misused by its master was aging all of them quickly.

"Will they sell us all?" asked Betha. Maru could tell the girl hoped anything would be better than Lorland.

"If we knew where they were taking us, we could make plans to escape," said another woman.

"Best just live in the moment," said Darlow. "We are alive for another day."

Lorland had Maru brought to his presence that afternoon. He was dining, and he indicated she should sit. She sat.

"What is your name and clan?"

"Minnow, Trawn," she answered briefly.

"Minnow, what kind of name is that? They should have called you chum. I bet you attracted the fish." He laughed at his joke.

"And Trawn, they are connected to The Silnik."

"Tara, a daughter of our clan was mate to The Silnik," answered Maru.

"Hmm," replied Lorland pulling apart a chicken. "Let me see your hands."

She held them out to him. He turned them over in his greasy hold and rubbed callouses she had developed from her month of working lines. He looked at her tanned skin and bleached hair. He even felt the muscles she had developed in her arms, but when he went to grip her legs she stiffened.

He laughed at her. "That was probably a better test of your virginity," he teased.

"Yes, silnik," she said gently.

He stood suddenly knocking over his chair. "Do not call me that. I am a captain, a self-made man." He thumped his chest. "Not some superstitious nit supposedly picked by a fish."

"Yes, captain."

Stared at her, "Do you mock me?"

Maru kept her lips shut and shook her head. That seemed to satisfy him.

"You are as bad as that old blind man. Your father?"

Maru could not stop the tears. What if she had not talked Traru into taking her sailing? Would he not be still alive?

"He's long dead by now, so stop your weeping."

"Yes, captain."

She seemed to pass some test that only Lorland knew. He gestured to the man at the door. "Take her back to the women. Make sure they are all fed well and given clean water to wash with and clean linens to wear."

The others were silent as Maru walked into the holding cell. She shook her head. "I think we will soon be in port. He's ordered food, water and clean clothing."

No one except Betha looked particularly happy.

When the water arrived, the women were glad to wash away the two weeks of abuse if only ritually and don the fresh clothing.

The next morning, they pulled into a port. They could hear the noisy greetings exchanged between ship crews and the landers. At noon they were led up to the deck. Lorland pushed Maru to the end of the line. Another line of shackled men was formed parallel to their own.

Maru found Tranin. He had a few more bruises than when he had left *The Laughing Dolfer*. He signed the word, 'okay' and then the symbol for a question.

She nodded. He turned his eyes front.

They were paraded through the streets. Apparently, the other ships had already moved their human cargo and Lorland's was the last. And she was the last of the last, thought Maru. She held her head high, she was after all a silnik. She looked at the people around her and wondered how they came to be this way. How did they come to accept this way of life, this way of treating people, as normal?

The harbor had several empty slips. She noticed Lorland smile at the empty tie ups as they walked past. He was happy that someone was not in port, thought Maru. It was not much comfort, but anyone that made Lorland smile by their absence, could possibly make him frown by their presence. That made Maru smile. Lorland had enemies, besides herself.

The crowds were thick and jubilant. Lorland's crew kept a corridor open for the slaves. Many eyes in the throng were judging them as they passed. Maru decided it was no worse now than all the official functions she had attended in her life. She tried to relax and notice what was around her as they traversed the streets whose walls were a riot of bright colors.

They were herded into a stone building with iron barred windows. The men were sent to the left and the women to the right down a hall and into a common area. The door closed behind them.

"Well that part is over," said Darlow.

In the morning they were given warm water and soap to bathe with and freshly laundered white linen to wear.

Lorland arrived with a scribe and began giving the man notes as to the order he wanted the women presented. Maru was last again. Waiting was never easy, but she had much practice.

About mid-morning the jangling voice of an auctioneer could be heard through the barred window. Descriptions and prices where shouted out to an audience which periodically put in a shout for a bid.

The men, thought Maru, wondering where Tranin would end up. Perhaps death was simpler. No, she shook her head to clear the thought, life gave possibilities, bad, but also good, and revenge. She didn't feel she was a vengeful person, but she hoped her curse on Darlow's enemy would manifest itself while she could see it.

The bidding seemed to be over around the noon hour. Lorland strolled down the detention hall with a broad smile on his face. He had made money, decided Maru. He eyed the women and smiled again.

Maru turned her back on him and went to where she could feel a fresh breeze through the clerestory windows. There was nothing to do now. She didn't even know where she was except it was west and north of Grantoli by about twelve days of sailing.

When the extra guards appeared, the women murmured and moved restlessly. Maru located the spot she decided would be the end of the line and waited. The door swung open and they proceeded back along the path they had followed the day before. Halfway to the ships the column was turned to the right and they entered a large plaza thronged with people.

The women were led from a back-corner street across the plaza along a zig-zagging path towards a stage. This gave the clients maximum viewing time. All around were eager, hopeful buyers. The guards kept the crowd from touching the merchandise. Someone took fright and darted away from someone's reaching hands only to land in the crowd with more grasping hands. She began to scream. The guards slowed to get the woman back in line. Betha, decided Maru. This was not looking like the salvation for which the girl was hoping.

Their destination was a stage at about head height. The women were led up a set of steps and lined up across the front of the stage. They were left to stand there until Lorland decided the bidders had seen enough. They were led through a curtain to an area out of view of the rabble. Behind the curtain there was a cage made of iron rods. They entered, and the door closed. Someone had pulled a sail across the top to provide shade for those below. Maru doubted it had been done for the men.

The first woman was pulled from the holding cell. She went fighting. It didn't matter, she still went. Maru had thought the auctioneer loud when she heard him earlier that morning. Now the noise was deafening. It seemed to her that the bidding went longer than she remembered hearing for the men. It made sense that Lorland was putting his more valuable goods at the end to keep the crowd's interest. It was why she was the last in line.

The gavel came down one last time and the crowd noise faded to a loud murmur. Eleven more to go, thought Maru.

Darlow was sixth. As they took her from the cage a runner approached Lorland and whispered in his ear. Lorland frowned. He cut in front of Darlow who just happened to be preparing to step forward. He tripped over her foot and went sprawling.

Maru cringed wondering if Darlow would find the small vengeance worth the fist he was certain to turn on her. The woman stood her ground as the pirate scrambled to his feet. He did not stop or turn back towards her but smoothed his kilt and passed through the curtain and out of sight.

Darlow looked back at the cage as she waited. Maru smiled at her. Darlow smiled back. She was a beautiful woman, may she find peace, thought Maru feeling a chill.

What had been so important to Lorland that he had not noticed the affront? A moment later the auctioneer's voice rose above the crowd. And Darlow was ushered through the curtain. Maru was certain the auctioneer's tempo had increased. At the first hesitation, instead of cajoling the buyers on the auctioneer brought his hammer down and Darlow was sold at a price way too low compared to the other five women that had gone before.

The guards had the next woman out of the cell and through the curtain before the auctioneer had finished telling the buyer where to deliver his money.

Maru decided she was not mistaken. Something or someone had spooked Lorland and he was selling off the women at a furious pace. The buyers soon caught on that if they wanted a girl they had better not waste time thinking about it or the chance would be gone. The bidding became frenetic with calls trumping each other at a faster rate.

Back stage, Lorland already had the next woman ready to push onto the stage before the final stroke of the gavel. Now the audience was starting to get ugly as men felt others were being given preferential treatment and their bids were being ignored. There was a growling quality to the sound of the crowd. The auctioneer slowed the bidding down. Lorland made another dash through the curtain and the tempo picked up again.

Maru and a sailor woman named Ella whose hair had a reddish cast to the blonde were the only two remaining as the gavel came down on the eleventh woman.

"The sea be with you, Ella," whispered Maru to the woman as she was called to the door. Ella smiled.

At that moment a shout went up from the front. A name was being chanted as far as Maru could tell. Lorland had been about to push Ella through the curtain when he heard the chants and turned red. Then just as suddenly, the crowd fell to low, soft murmurs.

Maru waited for the auctioneer's voice to continue, but his next words were unexpected. "Sorry, men. There will be a small delay while protocols are worked out.

Perhaps one of those empty berths in the harbor was no longer empty, thought Maru with a smile. It did not necessarily mean anything good for her per se, but Lorland was unhappy and that had to be bad for him.

Through the doorway stepped a sailor with a swagger that bested Lorland's. No, she was mistaken, a silnik, for the man wore a scarlet sash at his waist. He was probably as well muscled as her cousin, so not a silnik who let others do all the heavy pulling on the lines. His blonde hair was long and worn loose down his back. His eyes were a piercing blue very light even by sailor standards, but the nose.

Something about the nose was just unsailor-like. It was not an ugly nose, but not long and thin like most sailors, rather slightly snubbed. He was smiling as he parted the curtains. It gave him a boyish look that went with the swagger and smile. As he let the curtain dropped so did the smile. The eyes found Lorland. Behind him came a dozen large sailors who looked very capable as they fanned out around their silnik. And she noted all the men were armed with swords which for the moment were not drawn.

Lorland still had Ella's arm. He dropped it and came towards the new man with a broad smile.

The conversation was kept low, so Maru was not able to make out the words, but from the groveling Lorland was doing and the way the silnik's eyes were focused on the captain, there seemed to be a reckoning due.

Lorland gestured towards Ella who waited with head dipped.

Lorland seemed to be selling the woman's virtues to the newcomer, lifting her hair to let it shine like a copper coin in the sun and holding it to his nose as if it smelled of roses.

The silnik listened patiently and then turned to look straight at Maru. He said a couple of words and Lorland seemed to notice that Maru remained.

'Oh her,' Maru made up a dialogue in her head to accompany Lorland's movements, 'old fish, diseased, has clap you know, only here because I promised my mother I would get rid of her.'

The silnik's eyes did not shift but she saw his left hand make a gesture out of Lorland's sight. It was a clan sign, but for what exactly she did not know. The men stiffened and rested their hands on their sword hilts. Well, now she did know and put the symbol in her memory.

Lorland did not miss the sailors' readiness.

The silnik held up a hand to stop the torrent of words from the captain. He said a few words that Maru judged from the movement of the lips to be 'I will see her and compare.'

Lorland's guards had the cell door open and Lorland was calling her. "Minnow."

The silnik looked amused at the name as she thought she saw a smile tease the corners of his lips before disappearing.

Maru moved to the door. She watched Lorland and the unexpected silnik and found she was greatly amused to be part of the obvious discomfort being visited on the captain.

She took a place next to Ella and transferred her eyes to the back of the curtain.

"Your name is Minnow?" the silnik asked in disbelief.

"My family calls me so," she said.

"What clan?"

"I claim Trawn."

"You know Silnik Traru?"

It touched a nerve she thought she had buried. "The sea has claimed him. His ship Captain Lorland has claimed."

The silnik turned to Lorland. "To what ship does she refer?"

Lorland just realized another possession he might lose. "A small fisher vessel we took as we left Grantoli. The old man was killed and dropped overboard."

"Silnik Traru was your father?"

Maru nodded, hoping it would not count as evil against her to deny her own father, but Traru had been as much father as uncle.

"I had looked forward to meeting him. I am sorry," he said it with what Maru thought was true feeling.

He looked at her closely. "How old are you?"

"Twenty," she answered.

"You told me fourteen!" said Lorland angrily.

"Shut up, Lorland. If she grew up with a silnik for a father, she knows they can tell when people are lying."

At the mention of the word silnik, Maru could see that dangerous gleam of resentment creep into Lorland's eyes.

"Now she'll tell me she's not a virgin!" spat Lorland moving towards her as he could hardly take his anger out on the silnik.

"Are you?" asked the silnik, stopping the captain's advance. The newcomer watched her closely.

"Yes," said Maru.

The silnik smiled. Then the smile widened into a grin. He shook his head slowly in admiration and stepped back to look at her from head to toe.

"Well, Lorland, I could almost overlook your abandoning me and trying to sell off the catch before I could get back here. If I hadn't expected a double cross by your stinking hide I would, as you planned, have missed this."

"I was going to give you your share in coin."

"That was not our bargain. I was to have a fourth in kind."

"But they are all sold off."

"Except these two," reminded the silnik.

"And *the Laughing Dolfer*," uttered Maru.

Lorland turned redder and took a step towards her. "I claimed it."

"It was not salvage to be claimed," said Maru not flinching at the man's anger.

The silnik laughed. "But it is now, Minnow. Silnik Traru had to have been your father. No one else would have produced a daughter as ballsy!"

He turned to look at Ella who had been very willing to let the conversation not center around her. He looked at the red-hair and frowned slightly. "I would be within my rights to claim both of them and the ship, Lorland. But I'm feeling generous. I'll take the virgin and you can give me the rest of my part in coin."

"But I told certain buyers to be here," said Lorland breaking into a sweat.

"You also told me I would have a fourth of the items in kind," the silnik's voice had dropped and his men were tensing again. Maru was trying to decide the best place to move Ella if the swords were drawn and a fight began. "Be content that I did not go in front of the stage and tell them of your double dealing. No one would trust your word again, Captain Lorland."

Maru pulled Ella back a step at the iciness of the last two words. Lorland's anger grew but his math was good enough to keep it in check.

"Very well, Silnik Mahew," Lorland injected venom into the few words.

Mahew, thought Maru as she tried to position Ella so the men would have to go around her to get to the other woman. Mahew, a type of very treacherous shark.

The two men eyed each other as the guards were shifting slightly. Maru watched them as she did the best she could do to shield the red-head with her body.

Then the shark smiled. Maru did not feel any comfort in it.

"Partner, we should not come to blows over loot. I'll take this part of my booty now and expect a reckoning of the rest in coin in two days' time. And I will know exactly how much you made on this trip, Lorland."

He looked at the woman behind Maru's form. "She should make us a pretty penny, captain."

Ella knew her cue and moved around Maru to face the curtain. Maru touched her hand one last time in a gentle squeeze.

"Minnow," laughed Silnik Mahew turning to leave. Two men with him moved in to pull on her arms.

"I can walk without coercion," she said stiffly to the guards.

The men moved back slightly startled at her tone and Maru moved forward to walk behind the silnik. They exited the back stage down a set of steps far to the left of the stage and through another opening in the curtain.

Maru thought about the number of guards and the crowd. She could possibly lose the men, but she did not know this harbor and right now she was not chained. That thought made her think of Tranin.

"Silnik," she called to the man leading. They came to a narrow street with sunset orange walls that took off in some twisted direction.

He paused and turned to face her. "Fruits are not required to speak and are not encouraged to," he said but he waited for her.

"There is a son of Traru, Tranin. He was also taken in the capture of *The Laughing Dolfer*."

"Your brother," he stated.

She nodded.

"He could be dead by now."

"He was alive yesterday morning."

"And you want me to purchase him?" he asked in surprise.

"You seemed interested in Traru," she lowered her eyes, "I thought you might be interested in all his children."

"Not a lover?"

Maru looked at him in surprise. "Tranin? And I? Trust me he is Traru's son and my kin."

"And what do I get for rescuing your brother...that I don't already have?" He looked her over with an eye as covetous as any Lorland had used on her.

"Gratitude," she said meeting his eye.

"For simpletons."

"Now you sound like, Lorland," she said.

That he did not like. He moved closer and looked at her with narrowed eyes. "Traru should have taught his daughter manners."

"Men and women of the Trawn, speak their minds," said Maru. "Would you beat it out of our men? Then try and beat it out our women."

The man was taken back at her brazenness. "I should take you back and let Lorland's buyers have you."

"It is not too late I am sure. And after they tire of me, Lorland will buy me back for a lower value and have me for himself."

The sailor stood looking at her. "You are not afraid."

"Not after the sea," she said and remembered the cold. "Do as you will, Silnik Mahew. Tranin is here in," she frowned as she did not have a name for the place.

"Astral," said the silnik.

Maru nodded. Her spirits may have sunk a little lower. There weren't many places worse than Astral on Tienna's World.

"You know, it comes to me that I never did see the goods I just received."

Maru stiffened.

"Strip."

They stood in the middle of the street. Maru's fingers fumbled as they found the ties to the sarong she had fixed that morning. She let it drop where she stood.

"Your hands" he demanded next.

As she had for Lorland she held them out. The callouses had softened in two weeks but were still definite. He seemed surprised to see them.

"I should take you here and now then give you back to Lorland to resell," he said with a snarl. He stared at her waiting for her capitulation. She did not let her eyes drop from his. She was a silnik too, damn him.

Finally, he noticed her shiver from cold. "Pick up your dress." He took off.

Maru gathered up the cloth as the guards flanked her. She did not bother to do more than wear it as a cape over her shoulders as she hurried after her new master.

* * *

CHAPTER 9

Intare, he had long legs, thought Maru hurrying to keep up. She expected Silnik Mahew to turn for the harbor, but instead he began climbing higher into the port town. The buildings began to look cleaner, better kept if evidenced by their lighter and brighter colors. Individual structures seemed to fill the block between street corners, very grand indeed. Finally, well situated on the crest of a hill was a multiple storied edifice of rosy red walls. One of the guards ran ahead to announce their arrival.

The turquoise gate was open by the time they arrived. Maru was rushed through into a tunnel that opened into a mosaic paved courtyard. Mahew had not slowed and turned to frown at Maru's tardiness. He gestured with his hand for her to hurry.

The guards remained behind as they entered a second door at the top of a flight of steps that gave way to an opulent entryway. Beyond she could see a sunny atrium filled with plants that must be open to the sky above.

She looked around in surprise. It wasn't that Maru was unused to well decorated and beautiful buildings, she had been raised in a palace and most of the people she had ever associated with had money and taste, she had just not expected there to be anything this opulent or expensive west of Grantoli. Perhaps in the northern kingdoms inland, but not along the southern or western coast.

Silnik Mahew was smirking at her awestruck silence. Well, let him think her an unsophisticated rube, she thought. She was impressed, apparently piracy paid well.

A woman in a black wrap edged in pink came forward to meet him. Her hair was arranged carefully on her head. She gave Maru a disapproving stare. Mahew moved out of the hallway with the woman following. Maru decided she was expected to keep up and moved after them. She fumbled to rearrange her sarong to decently cover herself, realizing she had not made an auspicious beginning with the woman.

She appeared to be his housekeeper and was giving him an update of affairs while he had been gone. The two of them paid her no attention so Maru felt free to look at the various objects the silnik had collected as they turned into what must be a general living, entertaining space. It was a huge airy room.

There were shelves of books. Maru quickly tried scanning the titles. Most were commonplace enough. She had read or studied probably three-fourths. None of the rest interested her enough to wish to pick one off the shelf. A very nice clock ticked quietly telling time on the mantel.

There was a collection of knives, some quite old and several with hilts of interesting materials. She wondered about the balance and feel, but they were in a case and opening the door would have attracted attention and probably would have been misinterpreted. But now she knew where to find a weapon if she needed one.

There was a collection of fine ceramics. Some of which she recognized as coastal wares produced by centers along the southern and eastern coasts and quite old. She recognized a few that were rare items like ones her family owned. A couple of the dishes were clearly from Silton and had traveled many miles and centuries to be here. On the walls were paintings representing several ages of Tienna's World. She wandered closer to find signatures as she was certain she recognized one or two master artists from previous ages among the works.

"Minnow," ordered the silnik.

Maru decided she was about to meet the housekeeper.

"Yes, silnik?" she said moving forward with a smile.

"Holwon, this is Minnow she will use the usual room."

"Any special needs?" asked the woman eying Maru closely.

Maru was about to answer her when the silnik spoke first, "No, I do not think so. Give her the usual things, nothing special is needed."

"Do you think she will keep a daily hygiene routine, or should I assign someone to her?"

Again, Maru was about to answer, but was cut off.

"Let's see how she does on her own, again I don't think there will be any difficulties."

"Diet?"

As Mahew began to answer Maru decided they weren't talking to her, but rather about her. She wasn't needed, so she strolled away to finish looking at the painting she thought might be by Paulow. She listened to them continue to lay out their plans for her and went to look at another painting.

"Minnow!"

Maru came back with an inquiring look upon her face.

"You will remain here."

"Why?" she asked.

"Because this is about you," he replied crossly.

"About me, not with me. The conversation does not seem to require me."

The housekeep drew back in outrage. "How dare you speak back to your master with such insolence!"

Maru looked at the woman and decided she did not like her much at all. "I asked a question and made an observation."

"You are not required to perform either of those actions," said the woman with acerbity.

"When you are ready to talk to me or need me to answer a question, I will be happy to accommodate you," said Maru turning away.

The woman caught her with a firm hand. "You will stand until your master is finished with you."

Maru drew herself up and stood at the attention her father's guards had to perform for hours on end.

She kept her eyes front but could just make out the woman's face as it scrunched up in anger. 'Yes, I'm making fun of you,' thought Maru as she stood her duty. Mahew was directly in front of her and seemed to realize she mocked them both.

"Take her to her room," he said. "She is probably greatly fatigued from the day."

Well, he could cut with words.

Maru followed the woman up three flights of stairs to the upper levels of the house. The woman looked back frequently to make certain Maru was still there. 'You want obedience, you'll get obedience,' thought Maru with little love for the sour woman.

The housekeeper drew out a key and opened a door. "This will be your room. You will keep yourself ready for Silnik Mahew at all times. You will keep yourself and your room clean. Do you understand your obligations?"

"Yes, mistress," replied Maru wishing to add a few more comments, but deciding she had been lucky that day and the old bitch was only carrying out her job as she saw it needed to be done. She was probably in love with the silnik and resented the fruits, like herself, that were brought home for his pleasure.

"Do not interest yourself in any other aspect of the house or the silnik's affairs. You are here for one reason."

"Too bad I was a virgin," said Maru with a smile.

"It won't last," said the woman with an evil smile in return as she indicated Maru should enter the room.

"No, and you'll be glad when I am gone," Maru sighed as the door lock clicked behind her.

She stood and took in the room. It was larger than she expected, not that she knew what was the going space for a kept fruit, but it was as generous as her room back in Grantoli. For a moment she felt regret that she had run off from her family without a word. That had been cruel and if there was retribution from the universe at large, she would be asked an accounting of that action and perhaps the universe was about to require it of her if the old biddy's words were fully true.

There was a bed, of course, a huge bed, situated in a pink alcove, hung with elaborate ivory tapestries from a vermilion four-posted frame. The fabrics for the curtains and covers were embroidered in rich, deep purples and reds, both difficult colors to dye to that depth of color. A cushioned shelf at sitting height ran along two walls. There was standard lounging furniture. Chairs and chaises of cushioned comfort to match the other fabrics in the room. No hard, square, simple chairs, excepting one or two stools. Cushions piled on cushions were stacked in a corner. Honestly it would have been nice to see a hard-firm edge somewhere, she thought. Even the mantel over a fireplace that was not necessary in this southern clime, had a rounded curve to the edge. It all looked soft and yielding and compliant.

There was a wardrobe in a corner that was apparently part of the hygiene facilities that the housekeeper expected her to use. Maru opened it and found shelves filled with wraps of every color. Most were of sheer silk. A few others were the finest cotton she had seen. So transparent they were almost nonexistent. Nothing hardwearing or practical, she decided. She settled on a silk rectangle in sea blue with a purple trim.   On a lower shelf were slippers and sandals. She tried on several pairs until she found ones that fit comfortably.

Closing the doors and setting the wrap down she went to a counter where a pitcher of water and a basin sat next to a pile of fresh towels.

She poured water into the basin and using one of the towels proceeded to try washing the associations with Lorland away. What she would think of the shark in a few days she did not know, but right now it was enough to clean herself of one master.

Wrapping the silk in a conservative design she looked for a place to wait. Her stomach growled, and she realized her last meal had been the day before. She wondered if anyone would think to feed her. To take her mind off her hunger she wandered around the room looking at the decoration. A box held more cosmetics than she had ever seen in her life. There was a small chest on another table that she opened to find several decent jewelry pieces. Well any occupant of the room was unlikely to walk off with them, thought Maru, fingering the baubles then leaving them.

Nothing else in the room caught and held her attention. She sighed and moved to the shuttered windows through which faint breezes moved.

She attempted to change the angle of the shutters but found them firmly fixed. This left her with only a view at a downward angle. She moved her eye to the slit nearest the height of her vision. She had a clear view down to the harbor. She could see the dock area. Lorland's ship was easily seen and the two slips that earlier had been empty were now filled with two ships of equal size to the pirate captain's. At least one of those ships was Mahew, the shark's, she was certain.

Maru's stomach sounded its unhappiness. She frowned and looked for something with which to distract herself. She found some ribbons probably meant for her hair. She decided to practice knots.

When the light failed, and food had still not appeared, she tried to decide if the house's master had forgotten she was there or more likely the housekeeper, Holwon, was exercising her will to let Maru know that anything that came her way was due to the pleasure of the older woman.

Maru went to lie down on the bed but found it overly soft after sleeping for a month onboard *The Laughing Dolfer* and the last two weeks in cramped quarters in Lorland's holding cell. Between the sinking feeling of the bed and the cramping of her stomach she tossed and turned.

She sat up and looked around the room. The floors were carpeted. Grabbing a cushion, she found a clear area and stretched out. Her stomach protested once more, but Maru's tired body won out and she drifted into sleep, dreaming of her father, step-mother and the twins. Traru was there, Tranin also. No one pointed an accusatory finger at her, but they faded to gray and she was left adrift in the cold stormy sea and this time the dolfers were not coming.

* * *

CHAPTER 10

Maru woke staring at the ceiling trying to recall where she was. Her stomach growled, and she remembered. Oh yes, the shark's waters. She rose slowly. She took time to wash her face and comb her hair. Then with nothing left to do, so she sat. She found her foot tapping impatiently. She stilled the appendage.

Midmorning there was a click at the door that made her turn and focus her attention. She rose smoothing her dress. She was disappointed to see Holwon and that her hands appeared empty of food. She was followed by three women carrying buckets of gently steaming water.

The housekeeper looked at Maru's dress and frowned. Maru didn't know what was upsetting the woman. Her parents would have been pleased with her appearance.

The women transferred the water in the buckets to a vat high up on a wall. Maru had noticed it the day before but didn't understand what its use was. The floor under it was tiled and had what appeared to be a drain hole.

"Undress," said the housekeeper.

Maru bridled at the tone but acquiesced.

"Step over there," said the woman pointing to the area under the vat.

Curious, Maru did as she was told. One of the women pulled a curtain around her and another turned a knob. Water began to stream down upon her head. Maru looked up in surprise, then smiled at the warm rain of water on her face. She had bathed in tubs and occasionally taken cold showers in the summer, but this warm water version was much to be preferred.

One of the three maids, Maru couldn't keep track of them, handed her a bar of soap. She lathered her hair and rinsed it clean for the first time in six weeks, no salt water rinses this time. The water ran out and Maru found herself disappointed.

The three assistants approached with thick cotton toweling. Two had her body wrapped quickly and moved her towards a chair. The third began toweling her hair dry. The other two set trays and boxes on the table in front of Maru for Holwon's inspection. Maru knew from the previous night that they held cosmetics.

Holwon looked at Maru again and made her choices. The two women began applying a coating of flesh coloring to Maru's upper half starting at chest. The woman employed on her hair worked around the other two and starting at the ends slowing combed her way back to the roots to remove the tangles.

A mirror on the wall gave Maru a view of the effects of the women's work. The color they applied lightened the bronze tan she had developed on her uncle's boat. Maru did not approve but did not argue as the estimable Holwon was watching closely.

Maru's stomach decided to growl at them. The women stopped working in their surprise at the sound. Even Holwon looked shocked. They took turns looking at each other and then looked to the housekeeper.

She shook her head and they began again. Maru's stomach protested again. Maru smiled apologetically.

Holwon frowned. "Didn't you eat your breakfast?"

Maru answered, "I ate the evening meal the night before last." She had been too nervous to eat the food Lorland had sent them for breakfast the day before.

The minions looked horrified and Holwon looked non-plussed.

"Continue working on her, I shall check with the cook."

The moment she was out of the room, one of the women snickered. Maru watched her in the mirror and the woman saw her.

"Don't bring up her mistake, or she will make your life unbearable," was the woman's advice as she suppressed her delight at the housekeeper's error. She continued to massage the coloring onto Maru's back, working around the woman doing her hair.

"She's only going to double check that you didn't receive anything. If you did, and didn't eat, she will be upset and then she probably will forget to feed you deliberately," said the one smoothing out the makeup on her arms.

"She's not going to be happy with us knowing," said the third as she worked a tangle out of a lock of hair.

"We better not be caught talking to you when she does get back," finished the first coming around to dab flesh color on Maru's face and begin easing it onto the skin.

"What are your names?" asked Maru.

"They won't matter to you," said the girl working on evening the color on her arms as she switched to the other side.

"Either you will be gone soon, or we will," said the one looking at her in the mirror taking another lock of hair to straighten out.

"I see," said Maru. "Thank you."

The girl had finished her arms and wiped her hands on a towel. "Let me see your feet," she asked setting a footstool for Maru to rest her feet on.

Maru was feeling uncomfortable with the attention. "No one's ever helped me before."

"Silnik Mahew is very exacting," said the girl looking at Maru's coarse feet and sighing. "At least so says Mistress Holwon."

"How many girls does the exacting Silnik require?" asked Maru with more than some curiosity.

Two of the girls looked at the one combing Maru's hair. She shrugged. "You are the first in a couple of months." She sighed, "I'm going to have to trim several inches off your hair. How did it get so ragged?"

"Sailing," said Maru. Her stomach complained again.

All four women fell silent realizing the housekeeper might be back any second. Maru had no desire to make trouble for women who didn't seem to be in a situation any more stable than her own.

The three women continued their work silently now. Her feet were smoothed, and nails shaped with color added to them. Done with them, that girl began on Maru's hands. The maid had frowned deeply at the rough callouses of Maru's hands.

The woman who had been combing her hair worked slowly and methodically trimming the ends of her hair and then evening the results. In Grantoli, haircuts had been one part of her toiletry that Maru had been happy to have.

The woman applying makeup to her face had moved on past rouge on cheeks and lips and now was peering intently as she used a small brush to add coloring to Maru's eyelids. Maru sat quietly with her eyes shut and her face at a slight upward tilt.

Maru's stomach kept her from complete relaxation at the ministrations of the women. Just as it growled another time Maru heard the door open. Peering from her eyes she watched as Holwon entered with two women rolling in a cart. Maru could smell the food before the servants had the covers removed.

Holwon looked at the results of the handmaid's work. "The skin is still too dark," she commented. "Maybe the hair is just too white. On the whole it is better than we could have expected."

Maru opened her eyes completely to look at herself in the mirror. She was startled to not recognize herself. Not even a shadow of Maru, The Silnik's daughter, seem to look back at her. Well, maybe it was better this way, she thought. Whatever he did, she could pretend it was happening to someone else.

Her stomach interrupted her thoughts.

The two servants with the cart had laid a place-setting for one and Holwon indicated that Maru should move to the new table set for her. Holwon began explaining the etiquette and proper use of each utensil. Maru thought about deliberately eating with her fingers but decided she had antagonized the older woman enough yesterday and did not want the food taken from her when it had just arrived. She pretended ignorance of the different knives and spoons and let the housekeeper teach her how to eat. It slowed down her meal which was probably as well, for if she had not held back her knowledge of table etiquette, she might have wolfed down too much food in a little space of time.

She stopped well before her stomach was sated but decided any more would make her lethargic. Holwon frowned at what remained.

"Are you certain you don't want to eat more," she looked suspiciously at Maru.

"I don't think it would be wise to glut myself after the several weeks of thin rations," said Maru.

Holwon looked as if she was going to check her for plumpness like a chicken. "I suppose that is best. I will make certain that there is fresh fruit and cheese left here in case you are hungry between meals."

Maru blinked in surprise, "Thank you. That would be kind."

Holwon seemed to think there was more behind Maru's words. She nodded briskly for the remaining food and cart to be removed.

She had Maru standing as she hunted through the fabrics in the closet. She ended up with a soft brown silk with a gold ribbon banded edge. The women wrapped the fabric in gathers at her waist bringing it back around to the front and up over her chest to hang over her left shoulder.

The women cleaned the supplies away and left. Holwon nodded approval.

"Will Silnik Mahew come to see me today?" asked Maru with her eyes lowered.

"He'll come when he wishes," said the other woman shutting the door after her.

Maru went to look at the make-up again. It was beautiful but not her. She found the pitcher of water and a towel and carefully began removing the women's work. She felt cleaner, but now there was nothing more to do but sit and wait. At least she was fed.

* * *

CHAPTER 11

Another two mornings Holwon appeared with her trio of helpers to dress Maru. She was yet to be visited by Silnik Mahew, The Shark.

She could not get the idea from her thoughts of a mahew with its lazy trolling way of swimming until it decided to strike. A hazy, grey form just at the edge of vision under the water. Swimming with seeming disinterest that could change in an instant to ruthless efficiency when it decided to kill. She thought he had been about to strike Lorland the other day, but then the moment had passed. Maru thought Lorland stupid to double-cross this man.

Again, she wondered why her 'master' held off from visiting her, but then as she thought about her mental picture of the mahew, perhaps he had not yet decided to come in for the kill and until then he was indifferent. She shivered and wished the dolfers were here to surround her and protect her.

She smiled at the idea. It was known that dolfers would attack and drive off sharks, but unfortunately, her smile faded, one had to be in their environment for it to happen. She was left with the two-legged shark on her own.

Holwon was not warming to Maru. The woman was critical of her makeup, her posture and everything, including how much she ate or did not eat. Maru kept silent and submissive. As soon as the women left her, Maru would cleanse herself of the cosmetics and find a simpler dress to wear. The hair she left as it was easier than trying to undo it. The housekeeper did not appear to concern herself with Maru once she thought the girl was readied for the day.

Maru had to do something with her mind in the empty time she had waiting for the shark. She reviewed all the information Traru had shared with her. She checked the harbor from her slit view of the world. The two ships she felt had to be Mahew's were still in port. Why he did not strike was starting to wear on her. Perhaps it was the intention. He would not beat her down physically but mentally.

She sighed and found the ribbons to review the knots again.

Late that afternoon the door opened without preamble.

"You are..." the words died on the older woman's lips as she realized Maru's appearance did not match the ministrations of the morning. "What have you done to your make-up...your clothes!" The woman was horrified.

Maru did not answer. She thought the light green silk with cranberry red and gold trim very suitable. Her braided hair she had left with its ornaments in place. It was as elegant as any outfit her father had gifted her.

The woman looked around and then straightened her shoulders with a grimace upon her face said, "Get over here."

Maru stood and approached the door.

"Silnik Mahew requires your person."

Maru nodded and felt a pit in her stomach open. It seemed The Shark was indifferent no longer.

"I tried to make you presentable. If he is displeased it will be visited upon you," said the older woman with an angry glint in her eye.

"Yes, mistress," said Maru's lips, but with no contrition in her heart.

"Follow me."

Curiously they descended the stairs. Maru had expected the silnik would come to her room, or perhaps she would be led to his. But the two made their way down to the first floor where voices could be heard in the main room off the central atrium.

Holwon indicated she should wait as she went ahead to announce her presence.

Maru listened but could not make out the words. Two men and then Holwon's voice. A man responded. That would be Silnik Mahew. Perhaps he had decided to sell her on. Everyone told her virgins were a rare commodity.

Holwon was back with her blackest look and indicated that Maru should enter the room. Apparently, I am not at my best for sales purposes thought Maru with an inward smile.

Maru kept her eyes on the carpet as she entered the room. She could see three sets of sandaled feet and one last bare set that were rather dirty looking.

"Minnow," choked out a voice.

Maru's eyes flew up to find Tranin as the owner of the bare feet.

"Tranin? Brother?" she said stepping forward. She looked from her cousin to The Shark and back. She took another step forward and noticed the chains he wore. That stopped her.

"Stand next to him, Minnow," said the man-shark in a voice that made it sound as if the idea that had popped into his head.

Maru did as she was ordered, looking at her cousin as she did.

He had several more bruises than the last time she had seen him. He looked tired and was dirty. His eyes were worried, but he smiled at her.

Mahew was standing in front of them examining them as a pair.

"Strange eyes," he commented.

"Family trait," answered Tranin with more confidence in his voice than the overheard mumblings earlier. "Father's were brown before he lost his sight."

Maru squeezed his hand briefly.

The silnik studied their faces as if looking for some flaw. He finally shook his head. "Definitely related, even if the eyes weren't a give a way." He stepped back and looked at Tranin.

The Shark was deciding something, realized Maru feeling nervous for her cousin. She had pulled him into this mess and he was still standing by and protecting her in the only way he could, lying as to her parentage.

"Traru was a silnik," said the man finally.

"Yes, silnik," answered her cousin.

Maru realized Mahew wore his red sash.

"And you swam the Test also," he said as a statement.

"Yes, silnik."

Mahew turned and took a couple of steps away, deep in thought. After a few moments he returned and looked at Tranin as he spoke.

"Your sister put the idea in my mind that I should find Traru's son. An act to be rewarded with 'gratitude' I was told." He smiled at Maru and she swallowed.

He transferred his attention to Tranin. "I don't count on gratitude. I put my trust in other's commitments to bind them in ways they find difficult to ignore. But still it was an idea worth pursuing as it is often amusing and profitable."

He noted Maru's hand touching Tranin's. She dropped the contact.

"You would do much to protect your sister."

"Yes, silnik."

"Well, do as I, or my men direct, and I will promise your sister will not be hurt or sold."

Tranin paled. "I may be your slave, silnik, but I will curse you if you harm her."

"Harm is not what I intend for her. Are we understood?"

"Are we?" asked Tranin. "I promise, if she is harmed I will hunt you down."

"That will not be necessary," answered Mahew with a laugh. "But let me see if I understand what we are agreeing to. You promise to be obedient, and I will not harm or sell, Minnow. If I do either thing, you will hunt me down. Is that our pact?"

"Give me a knife and I'll seal my part in blood," said Tranin with a narrowing of his eyes.

"My blood?" Mahew laughed again.

"No, merely a blood oath."

Mahew opened a cabinet and picked out a knife. He tossed it in Tranin's direction. The chains made it difficult but Tranin caught it.

"Minnow, cut my palm to draw blood," he said handing her the knife.

"Tranin, are you certain?" she began.

"If he hurts you or sells you, I will kill him," answered Tranin with a venom in his voice she did not recognize.

She made a shallow cut and Tranin squeezed a few drops of blood on the floor.

"I am your man, silnik, as long as Minnow remains with you and unharmed."

Mahew tipped his head in recognition of the words. "Very well." To the guards he said, "Unchain him and take him down to the ship. Clean him up."

"Is it wise to unchain him?" asked one man.

"I hold his key here," said Mahew with a smile.

Tranin kept his eyes on Silnik Mahew as the men undid his fetters. He gave Maru a quick sign. 'Careful.'

Mahew did not miss the sign. Maru was not certain if he knew the meaning as signs could vary from clan to clan.

After his men left with Tranin he turned to Maru. "And now for the other half."

That was the thing about sharks thought Maru, you thought they were indifferent until it was too late. He moved closer and Maru felt turned on herself the intensity of the mahew when it was decided on a kill.

"You share more traits than just the physical with your brother. I want your willing cooperation just as I wanted his and I will bargain for it in the same way. Disappoint me and I will see your brother dropped back in that mine to which he had been sold. You saw how he looked after just a few days. They use up young men very quickly. They go in strong and are carried out dead or wishing they were." He let his words sink in.

"Cooperate with me and he will remain on my ship and be part of my crew. Disappoint me and I will destroy you both." She had not realized he had taken the knife back. It seemed as if a black mist gathered round the man as he made a violent slashing motion across his hand and squeezed several drops on top of the bloodstained spot Tranin had left on the floor.

She stared at the blood spot on the wood as it grew with each drop. It spread from the one small spot outwards in spirals. How could it grow and spread from such a few drops? She stared at it amazed as it turned into a gory whirlpool. Falling into it was the last thing she remembered.

* * *

CHAPTER 12

Maru felt dizzy. She opened her eyes and looked at her hands expecting to see blood. The only thing that color on her hands were the nails the maids had painted earlier that morning.

She looked around and realized she was back in the bedroom. How much time had passed? She went to stand and found her balance unsteady. She sat down quickly. Her head hurt. She reached up to touch a sore spot and found a lump that was very tender.

She struggled to her feet again and made her way to the window. Two ships were tied up. Tranin was on one of them. The thought calmed her. She made her way back to the bed and lay down puzzling at what had happened.

It had felt like the day she had blessed Darlow and cursed her enemies. But Maru had not done anything. Mahew had made the oath. Why would it affect her so and where had the whirlpool of death come from? Death...yes, many deaths, all sucked down into the maelstrom.

She heard the door open and sighed. He would want his 'cooperation' now. She calmed her thoughts and tried to sit up.

"No, don't get up yet," said a woman's voice. It was Holwon. Her voice wasn't pleased but she wasn't angry either. "Open your eyes and look at me," she directed.

Maru did as she was told.

Holwon nodded approval. "Better than before. What do you remember, Minnow?"

It was the first time she could recall the woman calling her by name.

"I was staring at all the blood and fell in," she said wondering why she bothered to answer the woman.

"What blood?"

Maru looked at her, puzzled, "All the blood on the floor, of course."

Maru looked down at her dress, "When will Silnik Mahew be expecting me?" She frowned at her wrinkled gown and started to pull at the knots that held it. "I need to change."

"Silnik Mahew is out," said the woman gently pushing her back into the bed. "He said to make certain you rested."

"What happened?" asked Maru wondering how there could be a whirlpool of blood in the house.

"You fainted and hit your head," said the woman gently.

"I never faint," said Maru with a touch of disbelief.

"You would contradict Silnik Mahew's word?" said the woman with a touch of her usual frostiness.

"No," said a tired Maru, "It is just so strange. I find it hard to understand it all. Why are the shadows coming at me?" she said softly finding it harder to keep her eyes open. "Do you know, Holwon?"

When she woke next the room was dark except for a lit candle beside the bed. She moaned and felt the lump on her head.

"Here, drink this," said a voice lifting her and bringing a glass to her lips. "How do you feel?"

"Worn thin," said Maru.

"There is food. You should eat," said the woman setting the glass beside the candle.

"You must love him so," said Maru closing her eyes. "And hate all of us in equal measure."

There was a sharp intake of air.

"I suppose, none of us are good enough for him," the girl whispered as she drifted back to sleep.

This time her stomach woke her. The light from the direction of the shuttered window was bright and she could hear the calls of the gulls and other harbor birds. She stared at the window for several moments before her brain began to sort out her thoughts and wonder what day it was and if there was food.

"Are you awake, Minnow?" asked a voice softly.

"Yes, Mistress Holwon," she answered perfunctorily.

"Sit up and eat," said the woman arranging pillows to support the woman.

"Yes," said Maru doing the woman's bidding but closing her eyes. "What day is it?"

"The seventh."

Maru went to shake her head, "I should have framed my question differently, I've lost track of calendar days. What phase of the moon?"

"New last night."

Three days lost to a bump on the head.

"Will your woman's month begin?" asked the older woman.

Maru laughed, "I am never visited by that which curses others."

"That is most strange," said Holwon. "Never?"

"When I was little my mother said it was its own curse as I might never bear children," said Maru opened her eyes as a tray was set on her lap. The aromas made her stomach growl. Maru laughed softly again. "You must think me continually hungry, Mistress Holwon. I swear I have had enough to eat in my life. It is only recently that I've been on short rations."

"You have not had food for three days; your stomach is good to remind you. Pay attention to it."

Maru ate until she felt tired.

Her eyes began to close. She fought to stay awake a little longer. "Tell our silnik that I am sorry to disappoint him."

Maru woke to find the housekeeper asleep in a chair pulled up next to the bed. Her face looked lined and much older than Maru had remembered. She reached out a finger to touch the woman's forehead. The woman started and woke up with a jerk.

Maru felt regret. "I am sorry, I did not mean to disturb you."

"It is alright, Minnow. How do you feel?"

"You know he will never abandon or forget you."

Holwon sat straighter and the muscles of her face settled into a frown. "A bump on the head has you talking nonsense, girl." She rose and crossed the room. "Do you feel ready to leave that bed?" It was said sharply but Maru felt it was truly a question and not an order.

Maru thought about it and nodded.

Holwon nodded and rang a bell. The immediate response was the entrance of the trio of women who had been grooming her since arriving in Mahew's house.

"Excuse me, Minnow. I will be back in a little while. Girls, look after her or find yourself out of this house."

"Yes, Mistress," they chorused.

"What is your wish?" asked the girl who usually did her hair.

"Everything but the make-up, please?" asked Maru as she slid her feet to the floor. She stood and waited for the room to stop spinning.

"It's been bliss downstairs with Holwon so worried about you," commented the nail specialist leading her to the shower. The others were pouring water into the vat.

"What do you mean?"

"Well she was up here, so there was no one to pick apart the work for flaws."

"The whole time," said Maru trying to recall. "Four days?"

"The master must have given her orders," said the color specialist. "He came out of the living room carrying you in his arms." The girl looked at Maru with a question in her eyes. "We thought perhaps he had hit you."

Maru shook her head. "Has he hit other people, women, before?"

"Holwon says no and we've never seen it, but it looked like it then."

"I...fainted. I think," answered Maru. "I don't remember. Tranin had made an oath and then Mahew had and then I don't remember."

"Tranin?" asked the hair girl as she stripped Maru's clothes away. "The slave the guards brought in. Who is he?"

"Silnik Tranin," she answered keeping a hand on the woman's shoulder for stability. "My...brother."

"Oh," said the maid and there was silence.

Maru looked at the women. "Oh?"

"Well, the silnik isn't known to like men and doesn't use any slaves on his ships as plenty of free men are willing to follow him, so we were wondering why he was here."

To insure her cooperation thought Maru.

"A silnik?" asked one of the women. Maru heard the question as the rinse water flowed over her head, "as a slave?"

"I've never heard of that," said one of the other voices.

Maru realized, neither had she. In the last free moments of *The Laughing Dolfer*, she remembered distinctly the other men falling or diving off the ship, but not Tranin. He had stayed. He had pulled on her hand when she would have tried to claw out Lorland's eyes. Traru had said that Tranin might be angry with her, but he would stand by her.

"Here wrap this around you, you are shivering," said one of the girls leading her to a stool.

Another one was looking through the wardrobe and returned with a very heavy silk fabric in a delicate pink. "This one might be the warmest. Put this one on her and wrap this one around," she said. They redid the simple braid for her hair.

"Thank you," she said quietly.

"Food should be here soon," said the shortest woman. She opened the door and looked down the hall. "We can cut you pieces of apple until then.

Maru smiled. "Just hand me the apple, please."

She crunched through the skin. The juices awakened her hunger. Tranin was alive and if she was obedient, he would remain safe. Her cousin would keep his word. But Maru was not sure if he would not try something to void the promise.

* * *

CHAPTER 13

Her days were back to the routine established before the fainting incident. The women groomed her each morning under Holwon's watchful eyes, then left her to wait. Silnik Mahew did not appear. She had been in the house ten days by her reckoning. It was too much time to think.

She wanted to pretend that he really wasn't intent on her; that she was just a valuable he had collected like the other objects in his home. Then she would remind herself that he was interested but was keeping to his own timing just like his namesake. She did not like that idea. Nor that she went by the nickname Minnow. It was only a matter of time before she would be snapped up.

Then the next morning Holwon spent an inordinate amount of time selecting the dress for Maru to wear. She finally decided on a blood-red silk with gold trim.

Maru had blanched at the color.

Holwon looked at it and then hastily put it back with an apology, "I did not mean to remind you of the blood."

Maru smiled and nodded not wanting to let the woman know the reason for her shock was the color was indicative of a silnik, the color of her sash hidden on *The Laughing Dolfer*. It made her think of Tranin, and with sadness her uncle and her father.

Once she was dressed and groomed the others left. Normally Maru would have rinsed off the layers of rouge and coloring, but today it was armor. Mahew would

have the creature they had created for him. She would hide inside and wait.
Minnows had to hide.

When she heard the servants with the dinner cart, she decided that Holwon was
mistaken in her assumption. Silnik Mahew was not coming for her today. She had
turned to stretch from where she was standing peering out the space between the
slats of the shutter at the harbor. The table was set. Her stomach did flips at the
sight of two of everything set neatly out on the surface.

She had just managed to take it in when he came striding in the door with those
long quick legs of his. He wore a dark red kilt with a patterned vest. His hair was
loose. He had his 'killer' smile on and even from here she could tell he smelled of
spices.

"May I join you for dinner?"

Maru could only numbly nod. His eyes were hungry she decided, but it was not
the food in the dishes they were looking at.

She sat across from him and could not help but notice the translucent silvery
hairs on his arms. His hands were large and finely shaped.

They ate for several moments before he finally said, "Are you always this quiet at
a meal?"

Maru looked up in surprise, "You're the first person I've had dine with me in
almost two weeks and before that I would not call those meals."

"I remember you were rather...chatty on our walk here."

"I..." Maru try to come up with the correct words. "I was still indignant."

"And now?"

"I am compliant," she said softly.

"Hmm. I'm trying to decide which Minnow I like best."

"Tell me and I shall be her."

"A little better and yet, not." He set down his fork and looked at her. "What have you done to your face, your lips?"

Maru touched the make-up. "It displeases you?"

"I did not say that. I don't remember you wearing such before."

"Well," she began carefully, "Lorland did not have any available, although we asked," Mahew gave a short laugh, "And the other time, I had removed what your maids had applied."

"Holwon had them do this?"

"To please you, yes."

"Does it please you?"

"I believe that is not the issue, Silnik Mahew. Your household seeks only to please you."

"Well, I believe it does not. Wash it off."

"Yes, silnik." Maru rose and went to the wash pitcher. She wet a towel and began to remove the layers of color so carefully applied. She opened her eyes to see what spots she had missed and noticed that he was watching what she did with interest. She shivered slightly.

"Are you cold?"

'I am sure you will find a way to make me warmer,' she wanted to say, but kept quiet.

"Are you cold?"

"A little."

"Come here. For Intare's sake I'm not going to bite!"

He felt the thickness of the silk draped around her body. It was wrapped as a skirt with the end length draped diagonally across her breasts to hang over her left shoulder down her back. It was very sheer, and the contours of her body were clearly seen.

"Do you have something warmer you can wear over your shoulders?" he asked.

"Yes, silnik."

"Well go put it on. It was bad enough you knocked yourself silly fainting, I don't need you becoming sick."

"Yes, silnik."

She found a wrap and put it around her shoulders.

He had moved away from the table to rest on one of the sofas. He stared at her. She waited with the wrap around her shoulders. She felt nominally more covered.

"You're still cold. Come here and sit beside me." He indicated spot.

She sat with her head submissively dipped.

"If your father is Traru, that makes you cousin to The Silnik's older daughter," he said at last.

Now Maru was chilled. She nodded.

"She must be incredibly beautiful," he whispered when she kept her silence. "Is she?"

"I have never thought on that," said Maru honestly.

"All the reports I have, say she is very lovely, but no one mentions you, her cousin."

Maru kept silent, worried that The Shark was too close to the truth.

"I only ask, for if you are this beautiful and no one mentions you, you must be eclipsed by your cousin, therefore she must be incredibly beautiful."

"My father kept me close to home," said Maru truthfully.

"I see," said Silnik Mahew leaning back to look at her. "Probably it was a wise thing. And I must say Lorland was clever to put you last, virgin or no. None of the other women would have brought anything like they did if you had gone earlier." He picked up her hand and turned it over. The callouses were not yet gone from her palms. He turned it over again and stroked the back of her hand and she shivered again. Compliant, she reminded herself.

"Still chilled?" he asked.

Her voice was caught in her throat. She nodded.

He motioned for her to sit upon his lap. She did so cautiously. He pulled her against him wrapping an arm around her to hold the fabric in place and warm her. Her head nestled neatly against his collar bone. It was comfortable, and Maru found herself relaxing a bit.

He chuckled. "You think me a shark."

She thought about denying it but changed her mind. Silniks could often detect lies as he had told Lorland. It was why she tried to tell as few falsehoods as she could. "Yes, silnik."

He didn't deny or protest and try to change her mind. He simply stroked her hair. The spicy smell of him was deeper and warmer with her nose against his neck. His skin was a deeper bronze than most of the sailors she had seen. His hair was whiter. He seemed to be more sailor than the sailors she could picture.

"You know sharks aren't much interested in minnows." There was a hint of amusement in his voice that had a soft seductive bass timbre.

"They will do in a pinch," replied Maru.

He laughed, "They are usually only interested if they cross paths, which wise minnows know to avoid."

"I guess I wasn't very wise," said Maru thinking of her insistence on learning to sail. She found a tear sliding down her cheek for her uncle and her cousin.

He looked down at her in surprise. "Shh, it is not that bad. I'm not going to hurt you." He laughed, "If I did, your brother would gut me before I knew what was happening."

"Forgive me silnik, I was thinking of my transgressions."

"You are not in the right frame of mind," he said with a frown.

"Tell me what you wish," she said clearing her mind of the mistakes of the past.

"Just rest," he said placing her head against his shoulder again. "Perhaps you were right not to talk at dinner." He frowned. "Everyone wants to talk, wants something. You want something. I want something." He sighed. "What a tangle."

"Yes, sil..."

"Shhh," he said resting his head against the top of her head. He buried his nose in her hair. "You smell of jasmine."

"If it..."

"Shh, it was an observation, not a criticism." He stroked her hair for several moments. Then he shifted to tip her face towards his. He bent over and kissed her.

It was soft and leisurely. Nothing possessive or demanding.

She pulled back in surprise.

"What is wrong?" he asked softly.

"I've never been kissed like that before," she whispered in surprise.

"Come, Minnow, I'm sure there were young sailors lined up to kiss you."

"They would not have dared my father's ire."

He smiled. "I see. And witnessing your brother's reaction, I can believe it."

He kissed her again. "Well?"

"As you wish, silnik."

"Come, Minnow, do I continue, or stop?"

She shivered, "Continue, please."

He laughed and kissed the top of her head then tipped her head to kiss her again. She had been right, he was finding a way to warm her. He kissed her eyes and she turned her head into his shoulder and he kissed her ear. "What else will you permit, as your father is not here?"

"As you..."

"No, Minnow..."

"I said I would be compliant."

"Answer my question."

"I do not know, silnik. This is more than I've ever done with a man." She whispered.

"Very well." He slid his hand from her face to slip under the fabric that nominally covered her breasts. He kissed her again as his fingers found the tips of her breasts and gently touched them.

She pulled back in surprise a second time.

He smiled at her. "Unpleasant?"

"No, but...different."

He smiled and bent to kiss one nipple. Her breath grew very uneven.

"Silnik, I, think, I..." her voice grew faint.

"Don't think," he said taking the tight little nipple in his teeth, then kissed it and straightened to look at her eyes. The look was bemused. "It gets better if you permit."

She nodded drowsily. He watched her as he slid his fingers around the folds of her skirts to find the moist space between her legs. She came out of her trance to grip his shoulder in panic.

"Shhh," he whispered brushing her lips with his and looking her directly eye to eye. He kissed her lips while his fingers probed the moistness and found that which he wanted.

She broke the kiss, gasping for air. "I...I..."

"Let it happen, sea foam," he whispered.

She moaned and went rigid with the unexpected pleasure and melted into his arms. She gasped at her oversensitive reactions as he continued to stroke her. She felt the intensity build a second time and again she found herself sliding down into pleasure.

He chuckled in her ear then bent to kiss her nipples that were hard and tight and so sensitive. He took the silk and covered her breasts. The stimulation sent her over the edge again.

"Please, stop," she gasped.

He held her for several minutes in his arms until her breathing smoothed out and she stopped trembling. She clung to him as emotions washed over her.

He stroked her head and buried his nose in her hair, inhaling deeply.

"So little virgin, did it please you?"

She pulled back to look at him. "But you didn't mount me," she said in surprise.

He laughed at her. "That will come another time. First it is important to know that there should be pleasure."

"And you?" she asked looked at him with that drowsy look in her eyes again.

He shifted slightly, "Perhaps another day. This will have been enough for you."

Maru sat up a little more alert. "You would give me pleasure and none for yourself?"

"Not all men are assholes," he said.

"I thought, I was here for your pleasure?"

"You do not think I enjoyed this?" he whispered. His blue eyes mesmerized her. He leaned towards her and kissed her again. She moaned.

"Do you want to give me pleasure?" he asked.

She felt a touch of fear but nodded.

He shifted her to perch on his knees. He took her hand and slid it down to where his manhood pushed against his kilt. "Touch me, kiss me." He guided her other hand to his chest and under his open vest.

She felt the tension in his body. His skin was deeply tanned, and his nipples were firm under the one hand. Her other hand found the shaft of his penis warm and pulsing at her touch. She kissed one of his nipples and he moaned. She stopped startled as his erection seemed alive in her hand.

"Don't stop," he said between ragged breaths.

She kissed the nipple again and felt the throbbing manhood. He suddenly arched under her and her hand came away wet. He pulled her tight and held her so until his manhood subsided to limpness.

"Intare," he whispered, "I did not plan to find release so quickly." He held her head with both hands and kissed her hair, then her eyes and finally her lips. He took her hand and wiped it dry with the fabric of his kilt.

He pulled her back higher on his legs to rest on his lap against his chest. She watched as he closed his eyes. His hand began a lazy stroke along her arm across her belly then down between her legs again.

She gasped as he found the center of pleasure he had stroked before. With closed eyes he smiled and touched her body until she found herself arching in pleasure and crashing at last to lay quivering in his arms. The smile on his face deepened. She fell asleep in exhaustion, sprawled across his chest.

* * *

CHAPTER 14

Three evenings of pure bliss and still she was a virgin. Virgin, but so enthralled to him that she waited only for his word.

After the first night they had moved to the bed and Maru found she slept the deepest and purest sleep she had since Traru's ship. She woke in the morning to his kisses and another quicker session of love making before he rose, dressed and kissed her good bye.

The women groomed her, their eyes curious, but with Holwon present they kept quiet. The housekeeper said nothing to Maru one way or the other that would indicate what she was thinking. Maru felt curiously happy. No one had treated her with such esteem except out of consideration for her father's rank. If she was to be a fruit, perhaps she could remain his fruit.

She did remember that the women had spoken of others. He was a shark, she a minnow and she would not make much of a snack for a man of appetites. She sighed. He had clearly chosen her because she was a virgin and was going to lengths to keep her that way. For this shark the hunt was what he enjoyed.

And it could only end badly for the minnow. He had told Tranin that he would not sell her, but he had not said anything about giving her away.

With her nights filled with love-making she slept for most of the days. It cut the boredom she had felt. Anticipation drove her stir crazy towards the late afternoon. She went back to tying knots to still her mind.

The fourth night he took her completely with her full cooperation. She was shocked as they climaxed together. He laughed at her and said that was the way it should be, but then he brought her pleasure two more times before they rested.

"Why do you make certain I am satisfied?" she asked as they woke, and he stroked her belly.

"Why should I not?" he replied. "Do you not feel happy when I am satisfied?"

She nodded.

"Then why should a man not feel the same towards the woman?"

"I suppose I've led a sheltered life," she said. "My parents were private."

"What would you share with a daughter about this?" he asked.

Maru thought about that. "Not to fear it," she said at last.

He laughed, "As a father, I would like to make certain the man was worthy of my daughter and would treat her well."

All those silniks that Traru had found lacking, thought Maru, and here she lay in the arms of a pirate one.

"And what will your brother think?" asked Mahew almost following her thoughts it seemed.

"You have kept your word. You have not hurt me or sold me."

"Will he consider your honor hurt?" asked the man kissing her gently.

"I think he will be content that I am happy."

"And so, am I." He kissed her lips.

Twenty days passed in exhaustive bliss. Then one night he did not come to her room.

She shivered in the bed, waiting to hear his key in the lock. The next morning, she was confused as she woke. She turned with a smile as she heard the lock turn.

Her smile turned to alarm as it was Holwon with the maids. The women did not meet her eyes as they performed their duties.

She tried to speak to the older woman, but the housekeeper finished and ushered the others out without a word.

Breakfast was tasteless. A thought crossed her mind and she ran to the shutters to look at the harbor. There was an open space at the docks.

He was gone, she thought, with a sinking feeling. She collapsed to the floor and tried to think what it meant for her. That he could care for her feelings in bed and then leave without mentioning his intent left her shaking with cold. She remained where she had collapsed, trying to think of other possibilities. The maid delivering lunch found her there and ran back into the hall to find help.

Maru could not find the strength to face them. She let them put her to bed but once there she turned her back on them. She shut her eyes and tried to sleep hoping she would wake and find it was a bad dream.

She woke to light and threw back the covers as she hurried to the window. The space was still empty. The hurt was deep, and she turned away from the window. Well, she had been compliant. She had just not expected to find her heart was more than compliant.

Now what, she wondered? She wandered to a chair and curled up in a small knot of legs and arms. She tried to make a tally of her situation. In the end she decided it was pretty bleak. She had gone from The Silnik's pampered daughter to a used fruit of a pirate silnik. In the process she had killed her uncle and possibly two other men and her cousin was as much a prisoner as she.

Now what was left?

When he returned, and she would have an answer before she decided. It was time to wait.

The first few days were not so difficult. The women maintained the morning routine of grooming and Maru had plenty of time to think alone. And she was angry.

At the end of the first week Maru was tired of thinking. Holwon and the maids did not answer the few questions she asked. The room had not changed. It had been lacking in interest earlier, it had not changed. She had just forgotten how boring it had been before... Tying knots was not enough to keep her mind busy. She was losing track of the time again. She would doze off and not remember if the women had come or not.

She kept a knife from the food cart without its missing being noticed. She used it to pry one of the shutter slats loose, so she could look up at the night sky. She spent the nights awake naming the constellations and keeping track of time. She would replace the piece in the window in the morning, so it would not be noticed.

After the women left she would collapse and sleep through the day waking for the meals but otherwise shutting her mind to any thoughts. She began to feel she was hallucinating as she was no longer certain what around her was real and what she imagined. Then she stopped caring about eating. On the rare occasion when one of the women would speak to her, she would look at them as if she did not understand what they were saying.

The moon waxed, waned and waxed again before anything changed. She was not certain what alerted her. The women did not groom her with anymore complexity or attention. Perhaps it was in Holwon's mien. Never very talkative, the woman seemed to be holding something back.

As soon as the women left, she hurried to the window. There lay a familiar ship at the dock. She smiled and sat to wait.

The next morning, they found her still waiting, asleep in a chair.

Four more days and Mahew did not visit her. She heard his voice echo up the stairwell once or twice, so he was in the house.

She would not beg, she decided. If he was not coming to her, then he considered it at an end. What it would mean to her future, she tried to avoid thinking about. It was all she could do to deal with the ache in her heart.

The fifth day started like the others. But late in the afternoon Holwon returned alone. She went through the wardrobe and located a gown made of heavy fabric.

"Put this on," she said helping Maru wrap and tie the dress with no further explanation. Holwon selected another wrap to place around the girl's shoulders.

Two men entered, and the housekeeper indicated Maru.

Maru backed away in alarm letting the shawl slip from her grip. She began to resist but Holwon came up behind her and placed a gag in her mouth before she thought to shout for help. The men tied her hands. She was tossed on the carpet and found herself quickly rolled up. Someone slung her over a shoulder and carried her out.

*　*　*

CHAPTER 15

Had Holwon sold her out, or was Silnik Mahew going to make her disappear and claim no knowledge of it to Tranin? Maru's mind raced through possibilities.

She felt her carrier sway as if he walked a moving surface. A ship, she was on board a ship. Had someone kidnapped her? If so it was likely to be Lorland but would Holwon do it for him? Perhaps if she felt aggrieved. Or had Silnik Mahew decided to sell her. She did not think it would be to Lorland. Somewhere else, somewhere Tranin would not be able to find her. None of this made sense. The only thing that was certain was she was being spirited out of Astral.

They descended a few steps and then she was dropped on a soft surface. A berth, she thought trying to wiggle out of the folds that enveloped her. She gave up in exhaustion.

She recognized the muted calls through the fiber as lines were cleared and cast off. Soon the ship seemed to sway and roll Maru from one side to another due to swells. Then the ship's sails must have caught the wind for the vessel's movements changed.

She wondered how long she would be left to wait. She fell asleep to the rocking rhythm of the waves.

The carpet being pulled away woke her. Roughened hands sorted out which way was up and stood her on her feet. The shoes Holwon had put on her feet earlier slipped on the floor as she tried to find her footing. The two men made no move to undo her hands or remove her gag. It looked to be dark out. She wished she could

see the stars to tell how late.

At some signal the two men stiffened to attention. The cabin door opened and

Silnik Mahew walked in.

It was not Holwon's plan, thought Maru. Of course not, realized Maru, the

woman was too loyal to the silnik.

"Untie her," he said simply. "And that will be all."

She chaffed the skin into which the ties had cut. Two months ago, she would not

have felt the bite, but after time in Mahew's household she had become soft again.

She watched him carefully. And he watched her reactions in return.

"Are you well?" he asked as if acquaintances on the dock meeting after a long

time. The shark seemed to circle in disinterest. She was not fooled by the shark's

indifference.

"Not particularly," she answered no longer feeling bound to honor her

agreement.

"Holwon did not misuse you," he asked with a frown.

"If you count abandonment to a room as soulless as a cell then yes."

He frowned. "Everything was provided, was it not?"

"Food, water, clothing, certainly. Conversation, ideas, thoughts, purpose,

apparently not."

"Why would you need that?" he asked seriously.

1She looked at him in surprise, "What was I to you? Only a partner in bed? Does a

woman not have aspirations and needs outside the small frame of a sexual

relationship?" The pent-up words came out with bitterness from years of a bland existence. The strict confinement of the last few weeks had magnified her situation and thoughts she realized.

He sounded aggrieved, "I was not demanding. *Everything* was provided. Tell me what you lacked!"

Maru struggled to keep her tone even and waited before she spoke, but as the words spilled forth so did her anger at her situation. At only being a woman. "Someone to talk with, something to do besides stare at nothing. Work, a purpose." She closed her eyes. "It was no different than casting me into a pit."

"You worked in your father's house?" he said with a sneer.

"I had some purpose and a role of sorts," said Maru remembering. "Perhaps it was not as strenuous as other women, but it kept my mind occupied. I am a sailor, not a hot house plant. Not a mindless fruit."

"What I gave you was not enough?" he asked softly. "The clothing was inferior? As your father's daughter you would recognize the quality. The attendants and their ministrations, unguents, oils, the care they took in tending for you, this was nothing? The food and room, were they too mean?" His face had lost its calmness. Something elemental seem to settle upon it. "The Silnik himself, could not have given his daughter things of equal quality!" he declared angrily.

"How was I treated? Like every other woman in the sailor clans. Chattel, a thing to be amused and dressed like a doll. A fruit has no more standing with a man than a free woman. Even the Silnik confines us to the land." It was true. No one looked at a woman needing anything more than baubles and clothes to keep them entertained. Her father had done no differently, even if he had made certain that she was educated enough to read for herself. "Even Lorland fed me and clothed me if not to the same degree, but is that living?"

"You compare me to Lorland?" he asked in a soft voice.

The Shark voice, she realized.

"Did I harm you?"

She shook her head, "Not physically."

"Then, damn me to Intare, what?"

She felt she was arguing with Tranin again. "I cannot abide staring at the same walls with no reason to live. It makes me...it makes me crazy. I start to not know what is real." She turned her back on him to survey the room. "You left without saying anything about leaving, where you were going or when you might be back. With nothing to do, I could only think. And my conclusion was that I mattered no more to you than any other slave or fruit."

"Why should I have..."

Maru shook her head. "Yes, why should you? You are a man as any other. It appears you have from me that which you wanted. So now you sell me off in another port to another master." she wanted to turn the conversation away from her state of mind.

"I am not decided. You could persuade me if you wanted." His voice almost purred.

She thought of the pleasure, great but fleeting and then the empty room, restrictive and suffocating. She shivered and shook her head.

"I see. Well, then I would not want you to feel purposeless in the meanwhile."

She had apparently struck a nerve with that comment. "I would be grateful for work," she said. 'As you are no longer interested in me,' she thought sadly.

"Most positions are taken, but I'm sure the cook could use an extra pair of hands." He had moved up behind her.

Maru nodded.

"And the decks need cleaning each morning." His voice was calm again and seemed thoughtful.

Maru nodded again. She could feel his presence, close and charged with emotion.

"And the men really need to have their kilts laundered on a regular basis."

With that job he meant to demean her, as most sailors only owned one kilt and if they were to be laundered, the men would have to go naked in front of her. "As you wish, silnik," she said trying not to let her anger show. She had asked for work.

Apparently, he was not satisfied with her quiet acquiescence. His fingers loosened the knots the Holwon had fixed earlier.

At his touch her skin tingled. She almost let the sigh escape her lips. She shook her head. He was only playing with her.

He paused. "Well then, what you are wearing is too fine to take such work," he said with an edge to his voice.

Suddenly she was alert to a change in the timbre of Mahew's voice that signaled the shark was about to attack.

He pulled the silk off her and threw it on the floor. "We'll see if the cook can find a rag for you to wear."

Maru looked at him in shock at the vehemence in his voice and action. "Yes, *silnik*," she managed to utter.

"And I think there is a place for you to sleep near the kitchen since you spurn my bed. Let us go and speak with the cook now." His eyes stared coldly, judging her reactions.

She nodded, too upset to trust her voice to answer for her.

The man exited the room. Maru followed numbly wondering how she had ever believed the man.

There was a cutting wind as they crossed the deck to the galley. The crew stared at her but not long as the silnik's face did not invite speculation.

"Cookie," hollered the silnik.

"Yes, Silnik," answered a voice from around a corner. A large man with hands the size of hams ducked under the hanging meats to enter the open space of the galley.

"I brought you the galley help you are always asking for." He looked at her coldly, "Such as it is." Mahew indicated that Maru should step forward into the light of a lantern swinging overhead.

Cookie looked at the naked woman in surprise. "Thank you, silnik. That is, does she not have clothing?"

"I'm sure you can find an old rag for her to wear. She is used to such things."

Cookie looked at the remains of Maru's hairdo and the paint on her finger and toe nails. "Are you sure she is up to helping me?"

"Yes. Keep her busy, I don't want to see her sitting anywhere daydreaming. And lock her up in the food stores for the night."

"I'll get a bedroll from the quartermaster."

"No! She is used to the floor of a deck. She is a sailor." It was said with a sneer.

Maru kept her head high. Damn the man to Intare. He had said men were assholes, she had not though he included himself in the condemnation.

"What is her name, silnik?"

"Minnow," said Mahew over his shoulder as he left.

Cookie chuckled but noticed Maru did not join him. "That's not really your name. Is it?"

"My family call me that," she responded with a shiver.

Cookie noticed. "I think I have an old blanket in my berth you can wear."

"Thank you."

"You should make up with him before you hurt yourself with a knife or hot kettle down here."

"Do I look that soft to you?" she asked feeling her anger grow. Was that all men thought of women?

"Seafoam, you look like some rich man's toy," he said leading the way to his berth in the back of the galley.

She looked at her soft callous-free hands then lifted her head, "I am a sailor. I am ..." she stopped herself before she said the words 'a silnik'. The dolfers had come, she had not drowned, and her uncle had said she would find strength for everything that came her way. She just had not realized that the strength took so much effort.

"Of course, you're a sailor," said the cook opening a drawer beneath his berth and searching it. "Anyone can tell you are sailor blood. But there are sailors and there are *sailors*. Here." He handed her a well-worn wrap. It was soft from use. She tied it into the most practical covering she knew.

"Now to bed," he said shoving her back towards the kitchen. "If it were up to me I'd let you sleep where you can find space, but since the silnik said the stores, into the stores you go." He unlocked a low door.

Maru thanked him and ducked her head to enter the space. Kegs and barrels were tied or strapped down to keep from rolling in heavy seas. Everything was tied down, except herself. She found a space where she could curl her body around a

barrel that smelled of fish. The ship finally rocked her to sleep.

In the dark of night, she was awakened by a shake to start her day.

* * *

CHAPTER 16

Her day started with swabbing the decks. It was a large expanse of board feet of which she was to become intimately aware. Sailors moved aside to let her clean. Occasionally a man would help by pulling a bucket of water up for her. But only when the silnik was not looking. She would thank them.

By the time she had finished the decks that first morning the sun was up, her hands were raw, and Cookie had breakfast ready for the crew. Cookie was off with a cloth covered tray to present to the silnik. The crew lined up and Maru ladled the porridge into whatever container was presented to her. She noted a disturbance towards the end of the line. Someone was continually being shoved to the back as new sailors arrived. There was no fighting, just shoving.

As the line shortened she could see Tranin was its end. The pot was nearly empty as the two men in front of her cousin asked for extras. Tranin stepped up. He looked unbruised if thinner than the last time she had seen him. She looked at the pot. It did not look as if it would half fill his container.

As she scraped the pot and took the bowl he offered, she asked softly, "Does he treat you well?"

"I should be asking you the same," Tranin said, his eyes narrowed in anger at the meager clothing she wore. "Are you sleeping with him?"

"No," she said, angry at the assumption.

"Then with the cook?"

"I asked for work. I am working." She frowned as she spooned the last of the porridge in Tranin's bowl. "Why do men assume women are only good for one thing?'

"It looks like he is trying to punish you." Her cousin took back his bowl and held her hand a moment longer to look at their redness.

She shrugged. "I let my anger get the better of my judgment."

A sailor pushed Tranin, "No talking to Cookie's girl."

At least he hadn't called her a fruit, but even so Maru turned the iron ladle on the man. "He's my family," she said with a threatening wave of the weapon.

The man looked from Maru to Tranin. "Family?" he said in disbelief."

"Sister," said Tranin. He nodded, "Later, Minnow."

"Minnow," laughed his accuser walking away with Tranin. "Your father named her Minnow?"

"She was rather small and shy as a youngster, but quick," she could hear him answer as they moved away.

The man's laugher drifted back to her.

Maru looked at the empty pot. Her stomach protested. She lifted the container and set it on the deck. She scraped what she could for her breakfast. It would not have filled a sixth of Tranin's container. Well perhaps she could ask Cookie for a biscuit later. They weren't very appetizing, but they would stave off hunger.

She went and pulled up another bucket of water and began to scrub the pot. Cookie returned as she was struggling to rehang the cook pot on the metal crane. He checked her work and nodded approval.

"Did the men all eat?" he asked her.

"Yes, Cookie."

"Even the new one, Tranin?"

"Yes, Cookie."

The man nodded. "There is a barrel of potatoes," he pointed, "start preparing them for the next porridge." Once he was satisfied with her start, he moved away. So at least the cook had an eye out for Tranin thought Maru with a smile. Her stomach growled. She nibbled one of the bad spots she had cut out of a potato. She was seated on the deck with the pot between her legs carving up potatoes when Silnik Mahew walked into the galley. She was startled and almost cut herself on the knife.

He smiled that 'killer' smile of his, the one he used when he was well satisfied that things are going exactly as he wished. "Well, Minnow, how is your day going?"

"Well enough, Silnik, thank you," she replied. "Tranin looks well."

He nodded and left.

She got to her feet and went to lift the cauldron of potatoes to the crane to swing over the fire pit. Intare, she had filled it too full. Somewhere she thought she heard someone snicker.

Maru ended up laying her wrap as the cleanest thing around on the deck, dumping more than half the potatoes on it then lifting the heavy vessel onto the crane and then transferring the rest of her work into the pot. She reclaimed her dress, glad that the galley was off limits to most of the men on the ship. She found her deck bucket and went to pull up water to add to the cook pot. She was tired, she realized, as she poured the water into the cauldron and shifted the crane over the fire. Life had been too soft in Mahew's house.

She found Cookie's supply of coals in a barrel in the stores. She carried a skirt full back to the ship's brick-lined cooking space in the galley. She raked the coals from the morning, making them glow hotter at the exposure to the air, then she placed fresh coals in a layer on top.

She wiped her sweaty face then looked at her hands and laughed at herself. The hands were black with coal dust and so probably now was her face.

Cookie stepped out of the meat storage carrying a side of fresh beef. He took it to a butcher block and grabbed a cleaver. "You might want to go wash your face," he said with a laugh.

"Yes, Cookie," she said with a tired smile. "What needs doing next?"

"A face wash," he repeated. "Take your time, the sun is warm today."

Maru found what she was starting to consider 'her' bucket. She pulled up another pail of water. She set it on the deck and squatted next to it using the water to scrub at her face and wash away her tiredness. Two and a half months since the raid had made her very soft. Even in Grantoli's castle she had run up the hill with the twins and maintained more muscle playing and lifting them than she had in the last months. That life seemed a very long time ago. She crouched numbly staring at nothing.

She took a quick look around. The men seemed to have left her to herself. She quickly undid her dress and upended the remaining water over her head. Not as good as the shower in Astral, but it would do. She tied the dress back around her wet body. Picking up the bucket she returned to the galley and her next job.

Cookie frowned at her as she hung up the bucket. "Did you eat?"

"There was some porridge left," she said not elaborating on how much.

"Biscuit in the barrel to your left. Eat one," he said gruffly.

She took one of the smaller pieces and replaced the lid.

"Can you cut meat?" he asked.

"I can filet fish, but, no, I do not know cuts of meat," she admitted.

"Just de-boning," he said with an expert whack of the cleaver. "The same as fileting." He hefted the cleaver again and chopped off another chunk of meat. "Throw those in the pot."

She picked up the bloody meat which dripped on her dress and ran down her arms. She dropped them one by one into the pot and returned to Cookie for the next load.

"Sit," he ordered as he continued to cut up the meat.

"I don't think the silnik..."

"He rules the ship, I rule the galley. If he wants to eat, he leaves me to my kingdom."

Maru found the stool and moved it to sit next to where the cook continued whacking at meat.

"What did you do to make him angry?" he asked accompanied by another thud as the cleaver cut through bone.

Maru sighed, "I didn't want to be ignored. To be a rich man's toy. Now he'll sell me I suppose."

Cookie eyed her a second and then chopped off another chunk of meat. "Can you apologize?"

Maru tried to think of what she might have done wrong for which she should apologize. She shook her head.

"You won't?"

"I don't know what I've done," she said. "He just walked out and then back without telling me anything and I've no idea what is going on."

"He was on business," said Cookie.

"And he could not have said good bye, I'll be back?" She rested her head on her arms that lay on the surface Cookie was using. The coals in the hearth were making the galley warm and she was tired. Occasionally the cleaver spattered her with blood as it cut off another piece of meat.

She fell asleep to the rhythmic thud of the cleaver. She woke to angry voices.

"I said she was not to laze around and I find her sleeping!"

"She had a busy morning," said Cookie's voice reasonably. "Minnow, come here."

She hopped off her stool and went to stand next to the cook.

Mahew's anger turned to alarm. "What did she do to herself?"

Maru looked down and realized her clothing was still smeared with the coal dust and now was spattered with the blood from Cookie's meat. Her hands and arms in fact were smeared with the blood from where she had carried the meat to the pot and it coated her face. Her hair felt stiff from the salt water rinse and probably stood out at wry angles. Even her perfect nails from the day before were chipped and cracked. He should be satisfied with her appearance she thought.

"Nothing, silnik. She's been very busy. The men get breaks through the day, I thought she deserved at least one."

Mahew drew himself up. "One. Only one, Cookie, or you can be looking for another ship." He stormed out of the galley in a manner not consistent with his namesake.

Cookie chuckled, "Looking for another ship."

"He would put you off?"

"The silnik?" laughed Cookie. "No, we know each other's secrets too well.

"Could you use some tea? I put the kettle on before the silnik came blowing in.
It should be hot by now. The teapot is in that upper cabinet," he said pointing. He
found a dry cloth to fold and use to lift an iron kettle out of the coals. "Tea is in the
box there, here is the key." He poured hot water into the kettle as she opened the
tea cabinet. Several sweet aromas greeted her nose.

"Which one do you wish?" she asked.

"Jasmine is my favorite," he confided with a smile on his huge face.

She found the container by smell and passed it to the cook. He uncapped the
glass jar with his large hands and with the same smile shook the loose leaves into
the teapot.

A few minutes later they were sipping their tea. Maru sighed as the warm liquid
slid down her throat. "This is a very fine leaf, Cookie."

He looked at her in surprise, "And so it is. How do you know?"

"My family has dealt in trade," she said.

"I thought Tranin said your father was fisher folk."

Cookie's mind obviously did not forget things, thought Maru vowing to be careful
with her words and confidences.

"Fisher folk sail far and wide after the catch. Sometimes he stopped at far
ports."

"What are you, Minnow?" he asked bluntly.

"A sailor," she said firmly and took another sip from her delicate china cup that
Cookie had served her tea in.

He looked at her. She sat primly she realized, sipping tea from a china cup like a
court lady wearing a bloody, blackened filthy scrap of patched fabric tied in the

simplest of patterns. Her face and arms were bloody. Her hair was standing on end from salt and the paint on her nails was chipped.

She laughed aloud at the picture she made. "What do I look like?" she asked him.

He shook his head and frowned. "Neither fish nor fowl," he answered. "You belong here, and you don't."

"Here, you mean on Silnik Mahew's ship?"

"No. I mean here on the sea."

"Oh, on that you are wrong," said Maru serenely. "The sea has claimed me." She sat a moment in thought then added pensively, "I just don't know what she wants me to do."

* * *

CHAPTER 17

Four days later was wash day. After the morning porridge was finished, Maru refilled the pot with water, cut soap into it and banked the coals under it. She found a wooden pole to help her stir the water and when it started to simmer Cookie hollered for the men to line up with their kilts.

The cook stood guard as the men shuffled forward to hand her their kilts and with bare buttocks quickly make off for another corner of the ship out of her sight. Maru pushed and shoved the wet mass of clothing around in the pot.

"Yours too, Minnow," said the cook.

Maru did as she was told adding her tattered cloth, spattered with all the cooking, coal carrying and bucket toting she had done. She picked up her wood pole to push the sorry scrap into the bubbling water.

"Here," said the cook handing her another fabric. "It isn't safe to work around the fire naked."

"Thank you," she said putting on the fabric.

"It is only on loan until the laundry is done," he said apparently needing to explain himself further.

After an hour of boiling, Maru carefully swung the pot crane to the side. She fished out sailor kilts with her wood pole and set them aside in steaming piles to cool before she would wring them as dry as she could twist them by hand.

The sun had been out but now it slid behind clouds that had moved in from the south. She hurried, knowing the men would work through the rain naked, but the kilts offered some protection. As she lifted the last cloth out of the dirty water, she began wringing out of the first of the fabrics piles. She shook and then folded the cloth and moved on to the next, leaving tidy piles of fabric squares in her wake.

Cookie was back and grabbed up the first of the finished laundry. "Come and get them," he shouted.

Men appeared from various corners of the ship claiming their garments. Maru worked as quickly as she could. The heavy wet fabric drained her energy and she found herself slowly until Cookie too was snatching up kilts to wring and handout without bothering to fold them. "Croaker," he called out flinging a still partially wet cloth at a sailor. "Jarn," he called another.

When the last kilt was gone, Maru found hers. She squeezed out the moisture she could. She exchanged the one she wore for the damp fabric. With the clouds hiding the sun, the brisk wind that had sprung up chilled her. That and her fatigue caused Maru to pause to catch her breath.

"Time to empty the pot so we can start supper," said Cookie with a grunt. He found dry towels and handed her one. Together they hoisted the pot from its hook and carried it closer to the side of the ship. There they tipped it onto the deck. The scudsy water steamed as it ran for the sides. Maru moved her bare feet before the scalding water found them.

After a quick salt water rinse, Cookie carried the hot cauldron back to its hook. Maru found the barrel of potatoes and started cleaning them for the pot.

"Don't you want to know where Silnik Mahew sailed when he left you?" asked Cookie wrangled a barrel to where he could open it. The contents smelled of salted fish.

"Pirating and looting," she said indifferently.

Cookie laughed, "Hardly."

Maru looked at him without much interest. She was too worn out to even think at this point. It was a situation she had wished for in Astral many days.

"We were visiting Grantoli," said the cook as he picked out fish.

"Grantoli," exclaimed Maru, surprise cutting through the tired grey she felt. "Silnik Mahew could hardly call in that port."

"Silnik Mahew, no." said the cook sorting fish and knocking off the extra salt.

"Then how?" asked Maru.

The cook smiled deeply. "He keeps a proper ship and crew and sails under another, proper name."

Maru recalled two spaces at the Astral docks. "So, he spies for the pirates?"

"I suppose you could call it that," said the cook pulling down his cleaver and chopping the fish into three pieces each. He pushed the pieces aside with the cleaver and indicated that Maru should add them to the pot. He selected more fish.

Two weeks there, to judge by the time it had taken Lorland's crew from her capture to Astral and two weeks back. That left maybe two weeks in port at Grantoli.

"But you're part of the pirate crew," protested Maru.

"Some of us can pass as proper sailors and some of us Silnik Mahew knows can hold our liquor and lips in port, the master shipwright, myself and Finley."

"He would not be pleased with your telling *me*," she said certain of her words.

"Who are you going to tell?" he commented reasonably. With another quick two whacks the next selection of fish was ready for the pot.

"What did he learn?" she asked irritated at the cook for the first time because he appeared to be correct.

"Grantoli's a mess," answered the cook as he picked his next victims.

"Because of Lorland's raid," she said transferring fish pieces to the pot.

"That and The Silnik is refusing to meet anyone, so our silnik did not get to see him and do business."

"Business?"

Whack, whack went the cook's cleaver. "Yes, *business*. Legitimate business."

"That does not sound like The Silnik," said Maru softly.

"Silnik Mahew has legitimate businesses."

"No, I meant The Silnik of Grantoli not seeing anyone," she said thoughtfully.

"It might have something to do with the fact, no one's seen his daughter since the pirate raids."

Maru stood quietly rigid.

"Seems she liked to take walks down through the harbor. The word is she probably got snatched by Lorland's raid. I can see that upsetting a father." Cookie's cleaver cleanly cut three more fish into as many pieces each. "That and your father, Silnik Traru, was pulled from the harbor and then thrown in chains in some prison."

"Traru...Traru's alive!" cried Maru feeling faint.

"Well he is for the present, but the word on the docks is that The Silnik stopped just short of hanging him and no one knows why." The cook looked at her. "Do you?"

She looked at him dumbly and nodded.

He waited, and she shook her head.

She had to tell Tranin. As long as Traru was alive...she closed her eyes and thanked the dolfers for her uncle's luck.

"That's enough," said the cook. It took Maru a moment to realize he meant the fish.

She found herself smiling at odd moments that afternoon. Once she was back in Grantoli, she would explain to her father and take the blame and Traru would be released. Once she got back to Grantoli...her smile would slip.

* * *

CHAPTER 18

Just four days later, Silnik Mahew told Cookie there would be another wash day. Cookie argued but acquiesced to his silnik.

"He just wants to make a good show as we enter Striden," grumbled the cook.

"Striden?" she asked, knowing they had sailed nine days.

"Home port," answered the cook. "It should be another day's sail."

"Silnik Mahew is from a western port?" she puzzled out. His dialect had not been strictly that of the southern sailors but she had not thought about it, had she?

"His home port," she repeated. He could sell her there easily to exactly the buyer he wanted. At least it would not be Lorland or someone likely to sell her on to Lorland, she reasoned as she cleaned and prepared the cauldron for the wash. The weather had been slowly getting colder. It was due to sailing further north she deduced. She would check against the stars if the clouds cleared tomorrow morning.

She emptied one last bucket of water into the pot and cut in what she thought would be enough soap. The coals had been stirred up earlier so the water was already starting to steam.

"I'll call the men," said Cookie looking at the clouds spitting rain at them. "The faster we can get this done the happier they will be."

The water was steaming as Maru pushed the first of the kilts under the surface. Once the men's were in she added her shift. Cookie handed her a fabric to wear without comment and she accepted it without comment. She was very tired this morning. Each day seemed to be harder than the last, she decided. Strength enough for what she needed she remembered.

The water began bubbling. The last time Cookie had insisted on a half watch long boil, but this time he looked at the pot and the sky and said, "Good enough. Pull them out." Maru began lifting the heavy, wet fabrics from the pot. Cookie disappeared. Once they were all out, she began wringing out the early kilts. There was not much use in folding them as it had started to rain.

"Come get your kilts!" she shouted into the beginning of the storm.

She wrung out sheet after sheet. Some of the men reached for their own kilt and after a cursory twist wrapped it around their waists and walked away.

Tranin waited. It was her first chance in days to speak to him alone. As Maru handed him the fabric she spoke quickly. "Cookie says Traru is alive in Grantoli."

Tranin stepped closer in the rain to hear her words. "What else?"

Maru sighed, "My father has him in chains. He is alive, Tranin."

The man nodded and walked away wrapping his kilt as he did.

Maru looked at the wet lump that was her clothing. She would put it on after she dumped the pot as what she wore currently was warmer and drier.

She found toweling to protect her hands from the hot metal handle. She almost had the pot off the hook by herself when the ship lurched, and the pot slipped off the crane to hit the floor and splashed its scalding contents everywhere including her bare legs and feet.

Maru went down in pain. She bit back the cry that wanted to leave her lips and pulled herself along the deck out of the hot water. She was whimpering just in the shelter of the galley when a looming shadow came out of the rain.

This time she cried out in fear and cowered.

"What the Intare!" thundered Cookie taking in the lobster red exposed skin on her legs.

"Silnik!" he roared into the wind. "Finley!"

The silnik arrived first. Maru had only a glimpse of his paled face before she shut her eyes to deal with the pain. "Finley, you wharf rat! Where are you!" Mahew hollered.

"Here, silnik," answered a quieter voice.

"Deal with her," said The Shark, leaving abruptly.

Maru whimpered as a hand touched her right thigh which had taken the worst of the spill. She could not stop shaking. "It will be okay," said a soothing voice. Maru opened her eyes to see what he was doing. The man kneeling beside her was not very tall by sailor standards and his hair was a violent red with curls that had been flattened against his head by the rain. Cookie stood behind watching, looking out for her, she thought.

"Breathe normally," he said laying his hand on her leg. "It will be okay. I will make it okay." She tried not to gasp ragged breaths but to slow them and control them. Her leg went from burning to warm to almost cool. She looked at what he did, but she could see no balm or ointment. He stared off at the wall behind her. He's riding the waves, she thought, recognizing the trance state she had seen her father use on occasion. Then she wondered if she could 'see' what he did or where he went.

It was like the dolfers, she decided as she felt a little of what he did. She tried to help him by sharing the energy he needed to fix her tissues.

After a moment he returned. He smiled at her and rose to his feet. He pulled her to her feet.

"Thank you," she stuttered looking down at the legs that looked a normal sailor tan.

"Certainly, dolfer caller," he said softly for her ears.

She blanched slightly. He winked at her and turned away.

Mahew was there with a cup of hot tea, leading the healer away.

"Silnik Mahew has interesting...friends," said Maru to Cookie, looking after the two departing men. She still was not sure how the healer had restored her so quickly. She shivered slightly.

"You need a big cup of tea," said the cook, beginning to pull her under cover of the galley.

She looked back. In the shadow of men ringing the galley opening she could make out Tranin. The men moved restlessly looking at her. Waiting, she realized, for some sign that she was alright. She raised a hand to them and found a smile. The men murmured and melted back into the rain and their various jobs.

Cookie pulled her towards his cabin. He sat her on his berth and pushed a mug of hot tea into her hands. She stared at him as he began to dig through a drawer looking for a dry wrap.

"Cookie, the silnik will not approve," she said thinking of how angry Mahew would be with the man with her.

"Drink" was his reply.

Maru looked at the tea that swirled in the mug, lifted her head to speak with Cookie and remembered no more.

* * *

CHAPTER 19

"How bad was it?" asked Mahew as he lowered the healer into a berth.

"You could feel it, Mahew. You don't need me to tell you." The man's face showed his weariness. "You never would tell about this Minnow. Where did you find her?" He took the mug of hot, sweet tea Mahew offered him. He started to take a sip then paused, "It's about time you tell me because I have some news for you."

He took a deep swallow and waited, watching Mahew pace slightly in the cabin space.

"Well?" the redhead prompted. When there was no response from the silnik he sighed and said, "I can tell you that you've tried hard to keep your emotions under control and I appreciate the attempt, but honestly you haven't done a very good job."

Mahew ducked his head and if the light had been better, he might have been seen to blush.

"She's the reason you were so elated the last time we were in Astral and..." Finley thought a moment, "She had something to do with the trip to Grantoli. And she is why you are so prickly, angry lately."

The red-head sighed, "Honestly, Mahew, it would be simpler for you and easier for me if you would just tell me." The healer took another swallow of the tea, set down the mug and slumped back in the berth. "You better tell me quickly as I am extremely drained of energy."

Mahew shrugged, "She was captured in the raid; I claimed her from Lorland. Her father is brother-in-law to The Silnik. I went to Grantoli to see what I could find out about her father. Turns out he is in The Silnik's prison. So, I had hoped to speak with The Silnik and get the man's release, but you'll remember Silnik Mertin wasn't seeing anyone."

"So now what?"

Mahew would have answered but suddenly Cookie's bellowing voice cut through the rain and the sounds of the ship. The healer sat up with a jerk. "Oh, the fool!" he said trying to stand.

"Don't you need to rest?" asked Mahew headed for the door.

"Come on, help me," the other man said staggering to his feet.

"Now what is wrong?" asked Mahew as they headed for the galley.

"I thought she knew what she was doing," said Finley.

"What do you mean, what she was doing?" demanded Mahew.

Cookie meet them at the entrance. "She's on my bunk in the back."

Mahew pushed past the cook. Minnow lay stretched out on the berth looking the cold bluish color of dead fish. "What the Intare happened?" he demanded.

"Damn if I know, silnik. She stood up, waved at the crew reassuringly. I brought her back her to get her out of the cold and find her something dry. I gave her the mug of tea but when I turned my back, she just passed out."

"Finley?" asked the silnik in an accusatory tone.

"She didn't allow for the energy she used, Mahew."

"What energy?"

"For the healing."

"You are making no sense."

"Didn't I seem to heal her legs in a rather short amount of time?" the young man quizzed, laying a hand gently on the still woman's neck.

"I just thought they were not as bad as they looked."

"They were bad, but she gave me a portion of her energy. Between that and the child, she overtaxed herself."

"Child? What child?" asked Mahew in frustration.

Finley looked up at him in surprise. "Your child I would judge from its feel."

Mahew drew back and looked at Finley and then the cook standing nearby. "I can't...that is...I don't expect to be engendering any children and you, Finley, know why."

Finley looked at the woman who gave a rather gasping breath and then was silent again. "No, she is definitely with child about eight weeks I would judge."

"Cookie?"

"Don't look at me, silnik. I didn't meet her until you brought her on board."

"Has she look or acted as if she were with child?" asked the silnik in exasperation.

"She did her share of the work. She was hungry but didn't complain nor ask for more than her share."

"Damn," said Mahew.

Finley looked at him in surprise, "You should be happy to be so lucky, considering it is not every day a silnik finds a suitable mate and one..."

The man was cut off by a lookout's cry. "Sail."

Mahew looked up.

"A greeting from Striden?" asked Cookie hopefully.

Mahew shook his head. "No, they are not expecting us." He frowned, "And few ships can catch us except..."

"Our own," chorused the men.

"The Moon?" quizzed Cookie.

"They had orders to wait in Astral. If it is the Moon then it is in Lorland's hands," growled Mahew.

"Two sails," called the watch.

Mahew turned but Finley stopped him. "Silnik, you have to know."

"Later, Finley," said Mahew as he pushed his way out of the cook's cabin.

"Silnik!

"Damn it man, I understand, she's my mate and she carries a child, my child..." he sighed, "our child."

"But there is more," said Finley taking a last look at the sleeping woman and hurrying after the silnik and cook.

Out of the rain appeared Tranin in Mahew's path. "Where is she?"

"Out of my way, sailor. We are about to be boarded."

"Where is she!" demanded the man again, the pouring rain slicking his hair to his head.

"Get out of my way or I'll slap you in irons." Mahew nodded at two sailors who each grabbed one of Tranin's arms.

"You need every hand that will support you, Mahew, I'll give you mine if you will tell me what has happened to Mar...Minnow," the man shouted at the silnik.

Mahew stopped mid-stride and turned back to the man being held. "What did you call her?" he asked puzzling at something just out of sight.

Finley had reached him and lay a hand on Mahew's arm, "Listen to him, silnik."

Mahew looked at Finley then back to the Tranin. "What name did your start to call...your *sister?*"

"No," sighed Tranin, "My cousin, Maru, The Silnik's daughter, Maru."

"A healer," added Finley, "although untrained."

"And a silnik in her own right," stated Tranin.

"No," said Mahew looking at them.

"Her father is The Silnik Mertin, and she called twenty-five dolfers of her own in front of witnesses," confirmed Tranin as the rain dripped from his hair.

"I was trying to tell you she can heal," said Finley, his words over lapping those of the sailor.

"Two sails closing," called the watch.

"And pregnant with your child," reminded Finley as the rain flattened his curls further.

Tranin's face paled. "Pregnant? It is unlikely she should be pregnant."

"Do not doubt Finley when it comes to the human body," said Mahew to Tranin. He looked at the two sailors holding Tranin, "Let him go and you never heard any business about her being The Silnik's daughter."

Mahew shouted to the waiting sailors, "To arms!" He turned to Tranin, "Find a sword and fight for me, or for your cousin, it does not make much difference now."

* * *

CHAPTER 20

Maru felt adrift in the sea. The dolfers greeted her this time, but she could not make out their intentions.

She woke to angry voices and the sound of steel on steel. She finally recognized she was in Cookie's berth, but why she did not remember. The sound of steel interrupted her thoughts and she paled wondering if Tranin had done something misguided like lead a mutiny. Someone must have landed on the deck above as she heard a rather loud thud.

She moved cautiously to the galley and looked around the corner. A sailor with his back to her faced Tranin with sword drawn. Tranin's sword was shattered but he still held onto the lower half. Behind him she could see Mahew facing another sailor, defending Tranin's back. So not a mutiny, decided Maru, reaching for the place Cookie hung his cleaver. She stepped quietly behind the man about to lunge at her cousin. She brought the cleaver down in an arc which would have made Cookie proud. It buried deeply in the man's shoulder and blood spurted as he collapsed, and she pulled the cleaver free.

Tranin stepped forward to take the man's sword for his own. "Get back, Minnow. Lock yourself in somewhere," he shouted at her. Then his eyes started from his face.

Maru found a knife at her throat. "Drop the cleaver."

She threw it away from her. It planted itself the calf of a sailor trying to get an edge past Mahew. He bent in pain and Mahew finished him off.

"Not exactly what I meant, fruit," said the voice in her ear.

The next words deafened her as they were shouted right beside her ear. "Drop your weapons, *silnik*, or I slit open the fruit."

Mahew turned wildly in Maru's direction and froze. Tranin parried a thrust aimed for Mahew.

"Give the order." The knife pressed against her throat and she tried not to swallow.

Mahew tossed his sword toward the side of the ship. "Drop your weapons," he shouted.

Tranin gripped his weapon tighter for a moment and then sent it after Mahew's.

"Well, Minnow, I did not think to find you in this catch.   This is the second time you have been found unexpectedly in my net."

She watched as one of Lorland's sailors tied Mahew's hands behind him and then propelled him to where Lorland still held the knife to Minnow's throat. He must be very frightened of Mahew to feel he still needed her as a hostage, realized Maru.

"I was disappointed to find the Minnow missing when I ransacked your house."

Mahew's eyes were cold and deadly and very much those of a shark, decided Maru.

"You deceived me on that score. But it has turned out in my favor after all."

"What of the others, those in my home and the men of *The Moon*?"

"Oh, the women are easily sold and the men...well the mines are always needing replacements." The knife stroked her throat. "And this one was supposed to belong to me from the start. So now we are even.

"Take him and lock him up. Who is the second here?"

Maru was surprised to see Tranin step up quickly. "I am."

"And your loyalties?"

"To Silnik Mahew."

Lorland looked at the man as if trying to place him. "Then you may join him.

"Any others with an overwhelming need to be loyal?"

Maru noted that Cookie and the young man who had healed her burns seemed to be absorbed by Mahew's crew and had disappeared

"Very well," said Lorland. "Lock them up below."

The knife was removed from her neck but the grip on her upper arm remained. "Let us see where you've been sleeping of late, fruit."

She was tugged along as he headed for the silnik's cabin.

It was as tidy as the night she had arrived except the bedding was rumpled. Her sarong was folded with the shoes set alongside on a shelf.

"Tell me you're a virgin still," taunted Lorland.

"I am not," she said quietly watching his eyes take in the room and rest finally on the berth.

"I should have taken you on my ship," he mused. "I just got greedy for the coins you would have brought me as a virgin. But now, it won't matter will it?"

He pulled her towards the berth. "Was he gentle?"

She nodded.

"The last time you'll experience that." He tossed her towards the berth. "Take off that rag and let me see what a silnik likes."

* * *

CHAPTER 21

"Why did you do that?"

Tranin ignored the question as he undid the ropes that restrained Mahew's hands.

"Why?" asked Mahew again waiting for the other to answer his question. "Why pretend to be my second? You could be out there protecting her."

Tranin shrugged, "I figured your second could do a more convincing job of organizing the crew for when they are needed if he was out there unrecognized. And as to helping Maru, I'm not sure how you think I could have helped her. Besides maybe you need someone who is familiar with the inside of this cell?"

"You are serious that she is The Silnik's," he paused unwilling to let any other ears hear the words."

"Are you serious that she is with...?"

They nodded at each other.

"Oh, Minnow," shook Tranin's head, "What happened to your plans?"

"Tell me about that," enquired Mahew as he looked at the bars.

"She convinced my father, as she could not convince her own, that she needed to be a sailor not just in blood. Only a month she said and then we could all go back, and she would explain to her father."

"What happened?"

"Well, it actually went very well, if you must know. She is sailor blood through and through. A month was up and Traru declared her a sailor and the other two men and I acknowledged her ability, but as we were to set sail back to Grantoli she insisted on the Test."

"Did she really call twenty-five? That is an unusually large number of dolfers. Maybe they were already there, and she just jumped in among them."

"No, in fact I think they must have come from some ways away as she almost lost the race with their arriving. She came out of the water more chastised than when she went in, but she called twenty-five."

"Your word counts for nothing as a relative."

"There were two independent men who witnessed and counted." Tranin shook his head. "I only called twenty, not that I'll tell her that."

Mahew snorted. "Only twenty?"

"What can I say, I was bested by my cousin, a woman. How many did you call, silnik?"

Mahew was silent then said, "Twenty."

"She thinks twenty-five is standard," Tranin grinned, "We need not tell her differently."

Mahew frowned, "If either of us get a chance to tell her."

"Is she pregnant or do you just hope to influence her father? The Silnik will know the truth."

"I did not know her connections. I only found out this morning that she carries our child and am finding it hard to understand. Begetting children is difficult in my family."

"Was the child conceived in rape?" asked Tranin his eyes narrowed in judgment.

"Rape is for those who do not understand women," said Mahew with contempt.

"Did you coerce her?"

"It was mutually positive," stated Mahew with a touch of bite in his voice.

"Then why abduct her? Why demean her to the crew?"

"As to the first, I did not want Lorland to know I had taken her out of the house in Astral." He paused. "As to the second...she irritated me with her requests."

"Requests?"

"I gave her everything she could possibly want, and she told me she was bored! That she had no role or purpose!"

Tranin started laughing.

"Why are you laughing?"

"Same thing she basically said when she made us take her sailing."

"It hasn't been boring since?"

"Difficult, but not boring." Tranin looked upwards in the direction of the silnik's cabin. "I am afraid she is reaping part of what she has sown."

"Damn the man to Intare," raged Mahew. "I should have cut that fish bait the first time I dealt with him."

"Does she care for you?" asked Tranin.

Mahew was silent. He sighed, "I do not know."

"Do you care for her?"

"I was taking her to my home in Striden," he said. "She would be safe with my family."

"And this before you knew she was pregnant."

"Yes," said the man sitting on the edge of a bunk. "I still don't believe she can be with child. With my child," he said with perplexity.

"I know what you mean. It was never easy in my father's family or The Silnik's either. Part of being a silnik I understand," said Tranin. "The last duty my father and I were asked to do for The Silnik was locate a suitable mate for his daughter."

"I am sorry to disappoint The Silnik," the pirate said with a thick layer of sarcasm in his voice.

"That remains to be seen." Tranin turned and looked at the other man, "Does she know she's pregnant?"

Mahew's face turned white. "No," he said softly. He turned as if searching the direction of his cabin.

Tranin stepped back as the other rose and words began spilling from his lips. Dark, ugly words that at the first hearing sounded like gibberish. Ancient words, decide Tranin, which coalesced into a miasma of darkness, filling the space, spinning around Mahew as if seeking something. Then just as suddenly the room cleared. Mahew blinked at Tranin briefly through eyes that could have belonged to any gleishen monster of Intare. Then the man's eyes rolled back in his head and Mahew collapsed on the floor.

* * *

CHAPTER 22

The first though Maru had as she woke to the pains of her body was that she had not been sympathetic enough to the women on Lorland's ship. If she had any excuse, it was that she just could not imagine people could be so bestial.

Her second though was that her curse on Darlow's enemies had either not been specific enough or lacked power. She lay there assuming Lorland was out checking out his other prize, Mahew's ship. Nothing seemed broken, but she felt terribly battered. She tried to shift her position and decided it was easier to stay put.

Earlier the healer had fixed her legs. Maru had seen how he had done it. She thought to try it on her body now to remove at least the pain. But she must have passed out this morning after the healing, the time she did not remember until she woke to pirates taking the ship. Fainted, as Traru had when he blessed her and as she had when she tried cursing Lorland the first time. If such things took that much energy, then she would be wise to limit drawing on that power until she really had a need. She would have enough strength to endure until then. She thought again of her uncle's blessing or perhaps curse. She was no longer certain. It seemed to work both ways.

Lorland had been very happy as he dragged her into Mahew's bed. His kilt had been grossly misshaped by his desire. But as he mounted her and reached towards a climax he had suddenly found himself limp.

He had ordered her to stroke and tease him into hardness and she did as directed. Again, he almost reached his desire and again he seemed to fail at the last moment.

He had slapped her then and shouted abuse at her. She tried not to cry out. He hit her again. The anger aroused his manhood and he entered her for the third time only to be frustrated again.

The last thing she remember was his punch. What happened after that she did not know except she seemed to have more bruises for which she could not account. Even drawing a breath hurt.

There was a knock at the door. She painfully pulled a blanket to cover her body from the person entering. It was unlikely that Lorland would knock first.

"Minnow?" asked the cook's deep voice.

She kept her face turned to the wall. "Yes, Cookie?"

"Are you hungry? Captain Lorland, ordered me to bring you some food."

Maru rolled over stiffly trying not to whimper at the pain it brought.

"A little," she said. She looked up to see Cookie's quick look of consternation. He put on a smile for her and set down a tray usually reserved for the silnik.

"Potato soup, my specialty," he said with a smile. His eyes looked worried. "Are you okay?"

"You mean, do I hurt as much as I look like I should hurt?" she said taking a sip of the spoon he held out to her lips. She swallowed carefully. "Yes."

"Don't worry. Silnik Mahew will deal with him."

"From a cell?" laughed Maru very briefly as even that hurt.

"He is a silnik, they have special powers."

Intare, she thought, I wish one of them was to be able to wish yourself somewhere else. "They are still only human," she said feeling it profoundly now.

The cook coaxed about half the bowl down Maru before she turned away. "I need to sleep before he comes back."

Cookie looked to the door. "Don't try the healing, Minnow."

She looked at the cook.

"Finley says you are not strong enough right now. He is usually right. Promise?"

Maru nodded.

"Your word," insisted the cook.

"My word, Cookie. Blood if you want."

"No, not your blood," said the man. "Is there anything I can get for you?"

"A damp cloth," she said at almost a whisper.

The cook moistened a cloth and brought it to her bedside. She went to take it from him, but he brushed her hand away and very gently wiped her face, pushing back her hair.

She found herself dozing off. The cook left the cloth in her hand.

She woke the second time to the door being slammed open. Lorland was standing looking at her. She could clearly see he was aroused but the longer he stared at her the limper he became. He turned away in disgust.

At the door he turned one more time. "See if you can pull your witch ways after I sell you."

Maru did not understand to what he was referring, she was simply relieved he had gone. She took the cold cloth and wiped places she could reach before the pain and her tiredness stopped her.

* * *

CHAPTER 23

"Food for the prisoners."

The guards looked at the bowls and spoons and let the cook through.

Mahew came to the grill, took the tray through the slot in the iron work and handed it to Tranin without giving it much attention. "What's going on, Cookie?"

"Eat and talk," said the cook. "They aren't going to let me leave anything behind and they might just cut you off before you finish."

Tranin handed Mahew a bowl. The man began wolfing it down.

"Minnow is alright for the moment."

Mahew frowned as he ate. "What is wrong?"

Cookie hedged and seemed not to know what to say. Mahew stopped eating completely.

Tranin's spoon stopped halfway to his mouth. "Is she okay?"

"Well, she will get better."

"Better how?" Mahew growled.

"He tried to..." Cookie shrugged

Mahew's features hardened.

"However apparently his member kept losing interest," said Cookie with a smirk. "The rest of his crew is talking about it very quietly, so I don't think you need worry about any of them trying anything behind Lorland's back or even with his permission."

"And Minnow?"

"Unfortunately, he blamed Minnow," said Cookie. Cookie tipped his head and shrugged. "Lorland wasn't gentle."

Mahew's bowl was trembling in his hands, splashing soup.

Tranin grabbed his shoulder. "One curse is enough for Lorland. You were out for half the watch with the last one. And from what Cookie says, it was effective."

"Curse?" asked Cookie.

"Very old, very elemental and hits a man like Lorland where his pride is centered." Tranin told him.

Cookie looked at his silnik with awe. "I thought the silnik powers were just knowing things."

Tranin answered, "Not always, Finley can heal. That is more than knowing things. Did Finley get a chance to help Minnow?"

"Finley will be holed up somewhere trying to buffer all the anger Lorland and his crew are creating," said Mahew calming some, "And probably feeling my own ire too. Damn, I don't know what my curse would have done to him."

"It is all Finley can do to keep food down. He was stupefied for several hours. Currently Lorland's rage is overwhelming him. He's pretty much balled up. I've got him hidden in the cook stores."

"What kind of silnik is Finley?" asked Tranin. "I don't know of healer kinds."

"Not a silnik," commented Mahew starting to eat again, "he hates water."

"What the Intare is he doing on *a boat?* With *you?*"

"He needs protection," said Mahew. "I provide him protection from...the world. He helps keep my crew healthy."

"If not a silnik, how does he heal?"

"He could be a silnik I suppose, but he calls it 'dreaming'. He can heal physical damage, and emotional hurts. His weakness is...he feels things too completely."

"Where does he come from?" asked Tranin. "He clearly isn't sailor-kind."

"Ask me his story later," said Mahew impatiently.

"I just wondered what part he would play..." said Tranin thoughtfully.

"What is the plan?" asked Cookie, taking back the tray.

"We've got to get off this ship. Preferably before we arrive in Astral or whatever Intare-hole Lorland has picked out for us."

Cookie kept an eye on the door he had come through.

"No chance to take the ship back?" asked Tranin.

Mahew stood in thought. At last he said, "Marginal."

Tranin sighed and nodded. "I think so too."

"There is something we are missing," said Mahew at last. "We need a ship, but if we did take back *The Silver Fish* and as fast as she is, Lorland would still have *The Moon* and she is fully capable of catching us even if his *Raven* isn't. We don't have enough men to take all three ships nor man them."

"What we need is my father's ship," said Tranin passing his bowl back to the cook.

"Were you not sailing her when Lorland caught you," said Mahew with a wry look. "Hardly a fast ship if he caught you with his leaky tubs."

"We sailed into his armada in the fog and had no chance to escape," retorted Tranin. "She's small but neither of your lumbering battleships could catch her if they tried."

"Peace," said Mahew. "I'd take your *Dolfer* if it could outrun Lorland."

"Ahem," said Cookie taking Mahew's bowl.

The two silniks looked at the cook.

"We were approached by two sails, but Lorland's towing a small craft."

The two men looked at each other and then Tranin stepped to the grill. "Get me the dimensions and appearance. If possible have Minnow look at it, she'll know if it is *The Laughing Dolfer*."

He stepped back from the grill as the cook left.

"Why would he bring *Dolfer* with him?" asked Tranin. "I will be glad if it proves true, but I do not know why he would do it."

Mahew was smiling. "I know why...Greed sees Greed. He's afraid to leave it behind."

"Someone else would steal it from him?"

"No honor among thieves," laughed Mahew. "Freeze in Intare, Lorland," he added with a cold voice fit for that place of icy damnation.

* * *

CHAPTER 24

Cookie was back sooner than Maru expected. He carried another bowl of soup with biscuit floating in it. The tray also held a large mug and a pot of warm sweetened tea. Cookie poured her a cup.

Maru felt well enough to sit up and drink the tea first. She shivered.

"Ahem," Cookie's voice reached her foggy thoughts. "You need to dress."

Maru looked down at her naked torso. "I'm okay."

"Here," he pulled clothing out from under the heavy sweater he was wearing. "Silnik Mahew needs you to look at something up on deck."

"Mahew?' asked the woman taking the heavy sweater and finding openings for her arms and head. The movements made her wince at the pain. The kilt she left for the moment as the blanket covered her. She shivered again, "Where is Lorland?"

"On the *Raven*." The cook noticed the girl shiver. "Here," he said again poured more hot tea into her mug.

Maru must have frowned. "Why..."

"He has women over there," said Cookie.

Maru shivered for her sisters.

"Drink more of the tea."

She pushed the mug away and realized there was a second question. "Why would Mahew want me on deck?"

"I'll tell you when we get there," said the cook taking the tea and handing her the bowl of soup.

Maru ate the soup as quickly as possible considering swallowing still hurt.

"Lorland isn't going to let me wander the ship," she said between bites.

"He hasn't set a guard at the door," the cook commented.

"Why not?"

"Where would you go? And I think he figures you are too cowed to leave the room."

"Does he?" she smiled slightly.

Cookie smiled in response. "Are you ready?" he asked as she wrapped the kilt.

"Yes." She grabbed his arm as she started to stumble. "Yes," she repeated more forcefully. He wrapped a gray cloak around her.

Maru wandered around the deck. Lorland's men, apparently having caught wind of how she had 'fixed' their captain and wanting none of it to rub off on them, avoided her. Mahew's men on the other hand made room for her to protect her against the 'others' she heard them whisper.

She mused privately that weren't they both pirates, varying in degree only?

Cookie in whispers let her know that Mahew and Tranin were both safe. Locked in a cell but unhurt.

"Why did Tranin say he was second in command?" asked Maru.

Cookie smiled, "So the real second could make plans." He looked slyly around to see if there were listening ears as he was about to add more.

Maru shook her head. "It would be best if I do not know of anything. I'm afraid Lorland would not have to beat me much to make me speak."

"You underestimate yourself, Minnow."

Privately she decided she had overestimated her abilities too many times to the detriment of others.

"What does Silnik Mahew need me to do?" asked Maru making certain they were alone.

"Lorland tows a smaller craft. He had the lines transferred to *The Silver Fish*. Tranin thinks it might be your father's ship. He said you would know."

"*The Laughing Dolfer* here?" she said with excitement.

"Look," said Cookie keeping an eye out for Lorland's men.

Maru looked over the side to find her uncle's ship trailing Mahew's ship.

Cookie looked at her face and had his answer. The cook looked over the side and pulled her quickly towards the galley. "Come to the galley."

"Now what, Cookie?"

"We wait until Silnik Mahew is ready." The cook made tea. He poured the steeped tea and added to her cup several lumps of sugar he usually hoarded from all comers except Silnik Mahew. As she drank her tea strong, hot and sweet, Cookie started selecting fish for the cookpot. She finished her drink, rinsed the mug briefly with a dipper of plain water then hung it on a hook reserved for the better ceramics. She gathered the chopped fish and carried them to the pot that already contained potatoes.

"What are you doing here?" accused Lorland stepping out of the wind and into the shelter of the galley.

She almost tripped at the sound of his voice. She gathered her nerve to look at him. "Helping the cook," she said, calmly transferring another load of salted fish pieces to the cauldron.

Lorland looked at her suspiciously but moved no closer. Maru was not certain if it was due to his recent impotence around her, or the cleaver Cookie used to whack a few more fish into pieces.

Maru gathered them and tossed them in the stew pot.

Finally, Lorland said, "Don't wander the deck."

"I'll keep her here, Captain," said Cookie seriously. "I'll keep an eye on her."

"Make sure you do."

*　*　*

CHAPTER 25

Maru helped serve the crew at supper. She could feel an ugly undercurrent between Mahew's men and Lorland's. She was not certain how long things would last as they were. Cookie pushed her towards his berth early and told her get as much sleep as possible.

She woke to a hand clamped over her mouth. "Shh," said Cookie's voice at her ear. "Silnik Mahew is ready for you."

"What's going on, Cookie?" asked Maru pulling the cloak around her and pinning it with the clasp the man handed her. He placed the strap of a bag over her head to rest on one shoulder. It was heavy and smelled faintly of bacon.

"Mahew's taking *The Laughing Dolfer*."

"What about Tranin?"

"He'll be there."

"Will you be the fourth?" she asked as they walked through the galley.

"No," said a voice out of the corner that led to the cook's stores. The red-headed healer was dressed warmly and carried another bag similar to the one she had.

Maru looked at him closely in the light from the galley fire. "I didn't thank you earlier," she said.

"You'll have time later," said Cookie moving out of the galley.

The healer indicated she should follow the cook.

Maru noted that the only ones who seemed to be around where Mahew's men. A fog had enveloped the ship. The sails moved lethargically overhead. Lorland apparently had ordered all sails dropped with the difficulty of seeing into the fog. Cookie's shape faded in and out as Maru hurried after him.

She found him huddled with two more shapes in the darkness. Both moved towards her. Mahew got there first and gave her a huge hug that made her wince. He realized her pain when she gasped sharply. "Forgive me," he said looking closely at her face and seeing the bruises. He kissed her gently. "Are you up to climbing lines?" he asked with apprehension.

"Tell me what you need me to do," she replied not certain how to react to his concern.

He nodded and turned to the red-head and shook hands.

Tranin hugged her more cautiously and asked, "Are you okay, Minnow?"

"I will be," she said with a smile.

"Over the side," said Mahew disappearing as he spoke.

"You next," said Tranin, "then Finley and I'll bring up the rear."

Maru looked over the side and could just see Mahew moving down a line into the grayness. All she had to do was hold on and she should just be able to slide down. She looked at the red-head. He looked nervous. Maru smiled, climbed to the rail and swung a leg over the line then lowered herself until she was suspended from her hands and legs that were wrapped around the line. She felt her muscles protest. She better be quick or she would be in the water and she didn't think she would float any better than she could climb right now.

The rope was slick from the fog's moisture and her hands began slipping as she tried to hold on. At that point she decided she should just let the pull work for her.

She slid until a pair of hands grabbed her and swung her onto the deck of *The Laughing Dolfer.*

Mahew studied her in the dim light and then kissed her again. "Start undoing the lines that connect us with *The Silver Fish.* Are you up to it?"

She nodded and stumbled towards a rope, focusing on his words to quell her confusion. She could see the healer halfway to the ship with Tranin just behind him. As she got the knots undone the lines sank into the water. As soon as Tranin was halfway she went below to stow the bag Cookie had given her. At the same time, she checked to see if her sash and knife were still there. She left the sash, but took the knife tucking it into her kilt.

Back on the deck she began untying the sails and checking the rigging. The healer was wavering as he moved towards her. Mahew was helping the red-head. Tranin was working to undo the last line they had used that connected them to the larger ship.

"Maru, look after Finley. He'll do whatever you tell him, but he's no sailor."

Maru looked at Mahew in surprise at the use of her given name, but the man moved on to the tiller.

A shout out of the darkness above made her lift her eyes. The red-head looked rather unsteady on his feet. "Go below," she suggested keeping an eye out for arrows.

"I'm supposed to help you," he said.

"Right now, it would be better if you are out of the way," she said unfurling more canvas and getting ready to hoist it at Mahew's command. Tranin joined her untying more sail, "She's right. You can help later, Finley."

An arrow bloomed several feet away.

"Let's get her underway and see how fast she is, Tranin," shouted Mahew from the wheel.

Maru pulled on her line hoisting the heavy canvas into the damp air feeling all her bruises crying for attention. Please, she thought, be enough breeze. They were drifting between two of the larger vessels. The third was blocked from view. More arrows dotted the deck.

Damn, thought Maru angry at the chips being put in her uncle's ship. She pulled harder. She was glad to hear Tranin was grunting also at the effort he was putting into raising his sail.

From the opposite side came an answering cry. They would be caught in the cross-fire she thought as another arrow planted itself just short of her foot. With the canvas raised, she ducked in time as the spar moved with the filling sail. The cries from *The Silver Fish* changed in nature and Maru could hear the clash of metal against metal.

"Get below," said Tranin pushing her towards the hatch.

"You need all hands if Finley is not to help," she responded ignoring the hatch and checking lines as she moved. "And we are almost out of range."

Another arrow planted itself between the two of them.

"Like Intare, we are," he said pushing her again towards the hatch.

Maru tumbled down the stairs hitting a wall and grimacing at the pain. In the darkness she could just make out the shadow of the red-headed healer.

"Are you okay?" she asked as she sat heavily on one of the berths.

"As soon as we get far enough from the fighting," he answered with short breaths.

Maru looked for kindling to start a fire in the brazier. Once she had it cut fine enough to where she thought it would catch, she found the flint and struck sparks. There was a small glow that she coaxed into a flame and carefully fed larger kindling until she could finally add a coal or two. Sighing she looked for the kettle. Nothing seemed to have been disturbed in the cabin. The only noticeable difference she could see was that someone had repaired the hatch damaged from when they had been boarded.

Overhead the sound of arrows hitting the ship had stopped. The noises of battle were fading. She snuck a look at the healer. In the firelight his features looked calmer. He noticed her attention and moved to where she tended the fire.

"I could take away the pain," he said softly.

"Not yet," said Maru. "It would deplete your energy, would it not?"

The man nodded.

"Then let my body heal by itself," she said reaching for a teapot and instantly regretting her choice. 'Idiot,' she thought to herself as she tried to ignore the pain.

She added plenty of tea leaf and poured the boiling water on top.

"Time for a counsel of war," she said picking up the teapot and two mugs. She managed the steps to the deck slowly. Finley found two more mugs and followed her.

Tranin and Mahew were arguing at the wheel. A quick look at Finley's face let Maru know that both men were not very happy.

"Tea, no sugar," announced Maru interrupting the two silniks.

"Beg pardon, Maru" said Finley, "I brought some from *The Silver Fish*."

Maru turned at the use of her name. Had everyone on the *Fish* known who she was?

"Why don't you and Silnik Mahew start while I talk with my brother?" Mahew smirked at her in the predawn gray.

Don't get angry, she thought. Finley doesn't need angry, but she could not help letting some of her control slip. "Tranin, how do they know my real name; do they know who I really am?"

"I thought it necessary as Lorland was approaching to tell Mahew." Tranin pulled the cloak higher around her shoulders. "Someone had to know, to look out for you if I could not."

"And you decided it would be Silnik Mahew?"

"Yes."

"Pirate Mahew?" she repeated. "Now he can sell me for more money or worse just demand whatever he is after from The Silnik."

Tranin looked embarrassed, "No, I don't think so, Maru. I watched him on *The Fish* when he was watching you. He is not indifferent. And a lot happened when Finley healed you and you fainted. You need to talk to Mahew."

"You might have heard, we are not exactly on speaking terms." Liar, she thought, remembering his kiss just moments before.

"Not from what I can see, Maru. You know his men had Lorland's outnumbered. He threw that away when Lorland had a knife at your throat."

Maru swallowed. "Are you saying he has my interests at heart?"

Tranin's features darkened, "Why do you think Lorland was impotent around you?"

"Mahew did that?" she said with disbelief.

"He placed a curse so deep and dark I would not repeat even a few of its words aloud, Minnow. Talk to Mahew." He headed back to where the teapot and mugs still sat by the men at the wheel.

When she joined them, they were discussing where they should go.

"To Grantoli," said Tranin and from the way he said it Maru got the feeling it was not the first time he had made that statement to Mahew.

"I agree," seconded Maru. "The Silnik should be told of where the pirates are and what is happening among them. Also, Traru needs to be emancipated from prison."

"There is something I need to do first," said Mahew firmly. "North where we were headed before Lorland arrived."

"We can come back," said Tranin. "It is important that The Silnik know his daughter is alive and well."

"Traru, and pirates," interjected Maru.

Mahew looked at them and shook his head. "I'll take care of Lorland and then we will see about your Silnik."

Tranin stepped forward but the red-head moved faster and blocked his passage to Mahew. He put out a hand palm forward. He held nothing as far as Maru could see.

Tranin gave the healer a puzzled look and went to move around him to get at Mahew who held the wheel with no concern for his person. When Tranin brushed the healer's hand to move it out of his way his face took on a strange look and he began to gasp as if he could not get enough air. Maru stumbled forward to catch him as he fell. In the dawn light he looked grayer than he should.

She looked up at the red-head from where she crouched next to her cousin. The man looked nervous and sick all at the same time. "What did you do!" she demanded. She looked at Mahew. Neither man answered her.

She turned to Tranin and felt into him in that manner she had seen the healer use on her legs.

It was as if Tranin wasn't there, or most of him wasn't there.

Mimicking the moves Finley had used in healing her legs, Maru lay her hand on Tranin's face and threw her energy into him.

"No," shouted Mahew and Finley simultaneously.

It was the last thing she remembered hearing.

* * *

CHAPTER 26

When Maru opened her eyes, she found she was staring at the ceiling of the cabin. Somewhere she could hear the men arguing.

"You better explain to her what is going on, Mahew." That was Tranin. So, he was okay, she thought with relief.

"He's correct," said another voice that sounded very tired. "She needs to hear it from you."

"We are still going to Striden," insisted Mahew.

"We'll go to Striden," agreed her cousin, "but I think it is a mistake."

A pair of legs descended through the hatch. Mahew's intense blue eyes caught briefly in the sunlight before he moved into the shadow of the berth.

"How do you feel?" he asked.

Maru was not interested in pleasantries. "What do you need to explain to me, Mahew?"

The man shifted in the small space. She could not see his facial features but the way his silvery hair ducked it almost looked as if he dodged a blow. She heard him sigh as he sat on the bunk across from where she was. His face was in deep shadow.

"And why must it be you?" she added her second question.

"Tranin says you are a silnik; that you swam The Test."

Moving sorely Maru found the spot to open the hidden compartment that held her sash. She threw it across the space at him. It used up most of her energy.

He fingered it gently and held it out to her. She did not take it.   He set it on the berth beside him.

"It is a talent to call the dolfers, like healing as Finley does."

"Or sucking the life from someone," said Maru hearing the cold in her voice.

"Finley would not have taken all the life, only enough to protect me," said Mahew. "But yes, even that. It is a gift, something the dolfers recognize and to which they respond. But there is a price for everything."

"To what price do you refer?" she asked thinking of her father's words.

"Finding happiness, having a family."

Maru could almost believe the wistfulness in his voice.

"Having children."

"It is long recognized that those the dolfers recognize do not reproduce easily," agreed Maru.

"And here we are, you, a silnik, and I, a silnik." He picked up her red sash again and held it out. This time she took it from him.

"Maru, you are pregnant."

She wasn't sure she heard him correctly. She found she was clenching the sash in her hands. "What did you just say?"

"Finley says you are pregnant."

"Not possible," she stated.

"Not impossible, just unlikely and just as unlikely, it is our child."

"How can Finley know if I am not aware of it?" she said accusatorily.

"When he healed your legs, he became aware of this."

"Aware how?" she wasn't sure if she was wishing to deny the possibility because it tied her to Mahew more tightly than she wanted or because if it was not true it would hurt.

"You could tell Tranin was missing that which Finley pulled from him."

"His energy, yes, but what does that..."

"How did that energy appear to you?"

Maru thought about it then replied, "Sort of greenish, like beach glass, but after Finley touched him it much clearer than I associated with him. It makes no sense to refer to him as a color, but it is as close as I can explain."

She could see Mahew's white hair nod in the darkness. "Finley sees us all as colors, or our energies as colors. Yours is a sky blue he says. Mine he describes as a shaggy brown. I'm never sure how brown can be shaggy, but he says that is the texture of the color to him." He let her absorb that information.

Then she knew what she had to do. She was indeed a blue, light and clear, but there in midst of her blueness was a small kernel of brown, not shaggy but rich with a hint of redness.

She came to with a start. "Oh Intare," she whispered.

The white head across from her nodded agreement. "You have to be careful. When you try to give your energy away, you take it not just from yourself. This is why you fainted both times you did so."

"You knew this on the ship?"

"Not until after you fainted the first time. Finley told me, but there was no time as Lorland picked that moment to attack."

"And that was why you surrendered your ship to him," she said understanding, "to protect your child."

"Not just it. I would have done it even if I had not known," he responded. "I had hoped to spirit you to Striden to keep you safe, not to sell you as you assumed. Perhaps I already sensed the child, I do not know."

"And Tranin knows also."

"He was there when Finley told me. I suspect that is why he gave me your real name and family."

"I must return to Grantoli," she said. "I cannot remain with you, with the pirates."

"I cannot let you go back," he said.

"The child may be yours by nature," she said, "But I will not let him be raised by you in this culture."

"I can keep you here."

"Yes, lock me in whatever stronghold you have in Striden until I'm a babbling fool," she said. "That's what you intend. Keep me safe, even from myself until he is born. Then you can take him and not worry about me."

"It is merely to keep you safe," he insisted.

"I told you how I felt about the room in Astral," she retorted. "You might as well put me in a prison cell."

"Maru, I promise I will not do that to you, but let me protect you."

"To protect your child."

"No," he said shaking his head. "Of course, I want it safe, but you first."

"Stop calling him an 'it'," she cried out and then found her cheeks wet with tears.

"Him...the child is a boy?" he asked in confusion.

"Finley didn't tell you that?" she asked archly.

She saw the silvery head shake no in the darkness across from her. He rose only to shift to where he knelt at her feet. "Maru, please, I fear for the future. I see shadows and I do not know what they mean nor how to change them. If we are meant to be mates, and my understanding is that only true soul mates can conceive, I want no harm to come to you, or to our son. Won't you let me protect you?"

Maru sighed. "Mahew," she shivered slightly, "I see those dark wings too, but perhaps there is no protecting, no hiding what you value...only fighting against that darkness and risking the precious, maybe even sacrificing it."

He had buried his head against her kilt, so she could not see his face. "You will not stop me from doing what I can to protect you and our son."

Slowly she touched his head. "Don't make it at the risk of my losing our son's father," she said softly.

* * *

CHAPTER 27

Two nights later it began to snow. In the lamp light Maru kept catching the flakes in her hands and then watching them melt. Mahew was amused but suggested she should go below before she got too cold.

"What is this?" she asked catching another drifting flake in the lantern light.

"What does it melt to?" he asked.

"Water," she said looking at her cold hands. "How can it be water? It is so different?"

"Water can be many things," he replied. "When you boil it does it not change into an airy substance?"

Maru nodded, "When it is hot."

"When it is cold it becomes this, snow, or sometimes ice."

I've read of these things," she said slowly catching another snowflake for inspection. "I never expected to see them. We are very far north."

"Or at least farther north than you've been before."

"I've only been in Grantoli," she said with a slight frown.

"Well, go below and add coal to the brazier. Your feet will suffer unless you have boots onboard?"

"No," she answered.

"Heat the cabin, we may all need to take turns warming our feet. By morning we'll be at Striden and I can get you a pair of wool boots."

"Why Striden? Why do you insist on it so?" she asked as he guided her towards the hatch.

"My family's home," he said. "There you'll be safe from Lorland. Go warm up."

When Finley came below to warm up, Maru took a turn above deck. The snow had stopped but a low fog engulfed the ship. Above she could see a full moon. The ship drifted slowly with the fog seeming to cling to the lines. Crystals began to grow on the ropes. The ship looked magical.

Tranin was at the helm. Mahew seemed to be checking the stars for their location. Dawn would not be many hours away, she decided.

A peak emerged out of the fog and Mahew gave a glad shout. "There, keep left of that rock, Tranin. We are almost there." His face was happy and for once looked relaxed.

"You will love them." he said with a smile.

"Who exactly," asked Maru.

"My sister, Betta, and her mate, Grend and their minx of a daughter, Brandt. You will get along very well with Brandt," he said. "You both are strong-willed."

"For women," said Maru pointedly. "You would not make that comment if we were men."

"Peace, Maru," he pleaded with a laugh.

She relented in the face of his happiness. The wind had fallen earlier when the clouds had cleared. If *the Laughing Dolfer* had not been such a light craft the zephyrs that existed would not have been enough to move her. They drifted through the fog in an eerie silence. It reminded Maru of some other place. When she caught the scent on the faint breeze she frowned and looked at Tranin. She could see he too was trying to trace the wind-born odor and identify it. It was smoke, but not that of heating fires. It was stale. She had smelled this before. Maru felt a cold that had nothing to do with temperatures.

The fog partially lifted as they drifted into the port. Snow blanketed the scene making it so beautiful in the still predawn silence. The smell of smoke was much stronger, but neither Mahew nor Finley commented on it. Maru was busy dropping the last sail then finding a mooring line. She jumped to the dock and slid as her feet skated on the slick unmarred snowy surface. She tossed a coil of rope around a post and pulled the *Dolfer* against the dock. A few coils more and she tied off the line. Tranin had done the same at front. They exchanged looks. The port was a silent snowy landscape, beautiful in a cold way. The fog teasingly hid the buildings in silence.

Mahew was chatting happily with Finley as he stepped to the pier. "Tranin, you come with me, Maru and Finley can follow." He started off.

"Mahew," called out Maru softly with searching eyes for the port, "Is something not wrong?" Maru looked at the nearest buildings. The windows looked like dark eyes watching them. Snow lay undisturbed on every surface.

For the first time Mahew paused and really considered his surroundings. Then with a cry he began running. Tranin was not far behind. They disappeared into the fog.

Finley seemed frozen to the ship.

"Finley, get two strong bags. We'll scavenge what we can find to eat."

"But," asked the man looking around as if waking from a dream, "where are the people?"

"Pirates, I would hazard," she said.

They found death. Maru did not take the time to give the dead much notice. It bothered her, but something internally kept her moving while casting a look over her shoulder. Something was growing in the dead port. Something of malevolent power. They needed to get supplies and leave. She doubted the pirates would return but it seemed wise not to be there if they did. Two stale loaves of bread were thrown into the sack with a leg of lamb. Two cabbage heads missed by the marauders was a great find she thought.

They had reached halfway up a street that Finley quietly said would end at Mahew's family home when they heard the sound. Maru did not know what kind of beast it was, but it made the hairs on the nape of her neck rise in recognition of some ancient foe. She found her knife at her waist and pulled it out. Finley dropped his sack and then ran stumbling and slipping up the hill into the tattered mists towards the sound. At the top of the street a dark gray shape came out of the fog and knocked the red-head senseless to the cobbles. It slid with the contact, changed direction and came rambling at her leaving a faint trail of blood behind it.

"No," shouted Tranin stumbling and falling at the same corner.

Maru stood her ground too frightened to know what else to do. The gray thing had silver hair that whipped around its lowered head. She thought it ran on all fours, and then was not certain as it seemed to rear back slightly to find her as if scenting the wind. It slid to a stop a few steps away with its pale death's face and gleishen eyes staring at her. Then it rose onto its two legs.

She could hardly recognize Mahew's features. The lips were pulled back in a snarl and yet moved in some incantation. The nostrils were flared back tasting the air. The eyes were dead and staring. The only color was the dripping blood from his left hand and the blood-stained knife held in his right.

His nostrils flared one more time as his head turned side to side as if confirming where she was. He moved forward one step then another.

Maru could not turn away from the dead eyes and the moving lips. Her body seemed as frozen as the ice they had lightly discussed. Snow swirled around them rising as a column on unseen currents changing colors as it rose into the rosy dawn sky.

She watched as he reached for her with his right hand. She expected to feel the stab of a knife, but his hand was empty. She saw his knife coloring the snow where he had dropped it, the source of the red tinging the vortex around them. He grasped her shoulder and pulled her roughly towards him. His lips continued to move in words too low to hear. The red swirled to black.

She was frightened at the lack of recognition in his eyes and squirmed in his hold trying to break loose. He brought up his bloody left hand and pressed it firmly over her face, cutting off her breath. She could taste his blood in her mouth and nose as she tried to draw a breath to scream. She choked on the hot metallic taste. Then the hand was gone but she found it slammed firmly against her waist as if he could push it into her body. She grunted at the impact. His face was inches from hers as he pulled her closer with his right hand and crushed his left forcefully into her midriff. His words burned around them, rising with the black motes, gathering speed.

The sound ended as if cut with the bloody knife at their feet. In the silence he let her go and staggered back a step. He lifted his head to the dawning sky and gave forth a sound that was equal parts a bellow of pain, rage, and sorrow. It rose into the clear pale sky startling birds from their roosts.

He dropped to his knees. The gleishen stared at Maru briefly before spewing hot bile onto the cobbles at her feet. The thing looked at her one last time with a faint suggestion of returning sanity in the features then its eyes rolled back, and it collapsed the rest of the way into the snow.

Maru stood trembling, her ears ringing with the echo of his words and wordless howl of pain. She stared at the lump at her feet. Shouting finally penetrated her awareness as she realized part of her quaking was Tranin shaking her. She blinked and looked at him.

He started to scoop her up to carry her. She broke his grip. "Take Mahew," she said as calmly as she could. She saw Finley trying to stand at the corner. "I'll help Finley."

"To Intare with Mahew," growled Tranin, "May he freeze there! He has hurt you!"

Maru paused then answered, "No, I think I am okay."

"Maru, it is the same as when he cursed Lorland!"

Maru looked at the crumpled heap that was the silnik they discussed. "Was it a curse?" she asked softly. "You father said it hard to tell blessings and curses at times."

"Leave him!"

Maru looked into her cousin's eyes as she eased his grip from her arm. "Help me, Tranin," she said quietly. She moved to Finley.

"Maru, we can leave him here."

"We need him," she reminded him as she helped the woozy red-head to his feet.

"We can manage," her cousin argued.

"We need him. The two of us cannot manage the ship alone even with Finley," she sighed, "but more importantly I need him, Tranin." She shouldered the healer's weight and turned for the harbor. She did not look back to see if Tranin followed.

* * *

CHAPTER 28

It had taken more time to convince Tranin that there was nothing wrong with her, that all the blood covering her was Mahew's.

"Put him in the cabin" she said as Tranin carried Mahew's limp form onto the boat leaving a bloody trail of scarlet drops on the wood of the deck. She did not have time to go ahead and help as she was shouldering Finley whose rubbery legs and pale face said he was close to collapsing.

She almost lost her balance as she tried to get Finley onto the ship over the gap. Tranin arrived in time to pull the unresisting man from her grip and then grab her shoulder to pull her across the watery fissure and onboard.

"Get Finley below. I'll take care of them. You'll need to go back for the sacks we dropped," she said following her tall cousin.

"We should get away from here," said Tranin with a glance for the bloody trail that led straight to their ship.

"No," she said slowly following his gaze, "Whatever was evil is gone now."

"Yes, down below," said Tranin curtly as he lowered Finley into the hold and let him drop to the floor next to Mahew.

Maru frowned at Tranin's heedlessness.

She took a step towards the hold. Tranin stopped her and looked again at her bloodied condition. "Are you sure you are okay? You are sure it was not a curse?"

"I don't know what he did, Tranin. I don't feel different. The baby feels okay."

"The last time I saw that face on him, he cursed Lorland to impotence," said Tranin grimly.

"What happened up there?" she asked softly looking back at the port whose snow was taking on a rosy hue in the dawn's light.

"By the time I got to him, he was clearing snow from the face of a man's corpse in a fire gutted house. Then he ran to another spot, sweeping away the snow to reveal a woman. I would assume they were his sister and her mate."

"What of his niece?" she asked as she swung a leg over the edge of the hatch onto the ladder.

"I didn't see anyone and the next thing I knew Mahew had turned into that gleishen thing you saw.

Maru looked up at her cousin. "Go get our bags. We need the provisions. And see if you can find me some boots, I can't feel my feet." She took a step down the ladder, "I'll make plenty of hot tea for when you return."

"You are certain that you'll be okay with...that thing?"

"Go get find me boots and anything else you think we can use."

She got Finley's form up off the floor and into a berth. The man's eyes were open, but his gaze was unfocused. She got him under blankets then turned towards the bigger problem.

Mahew was heavier and it took her several moments to get him into a berth. His face was bluish but not, she suspected, from cold. She got him under covers. This was not a time to thrift she decided as she placed coals in the brazier. She filled the kettle from the fresh water supply and decided she should send Tranin back out to refill that barrel before they left.

Finley groaned and then closed his eyes. He moved under the covering, so she decided not to worry about him. She turned to Mahew on the other berth whose form was still and gray. She touched his wrist to find a pulse. It was slow and his body very cold. She found his left hand and got it to where she could look at the cut in the light from the fire. Not too deep but still bleeding.

She poured some of the kettle water onto a cloth. It was nicely warm to her touch. She used it to wash the blood from Mahew's hand. She could trace a scar parallel to the wound he had given himself today. That had been the slash he had made back in Astral she recalled. The one that had her seeing blood everywhere. She suspected that not enough blood had been spilled yet.

She wrapped a clean cloth around his injury and tied it off neatly. His color was still bad. He had a pulse, but it was weak and slow. Maru had dealt with what she could see. Any other injuries he had she was at a loss to know how to deal with them.

Finley had calmed finally. Maru put more coals in the brazier as she removed the kettle to make tea. To the loose tea leaves she added as much sugar as she could dissolve in the hot water. At the sound of something dropping onto the deck she found her knife and inched cautiously to the hatch. She peered over the lip of the hatch to see an exhausted Tranin tossing bags onto the ship.

She filled a mug with hot tea and hurried to give it to him. In exchange he gave her a pair of woolen boots.

She pulled them onto her wet and dirty feet.

"Now what, Maru?" asked Tranin in a voice not unlike the one he had used on her the day she had kidnapped her cousin and uncle to go sailing.

"We can't manage the *Dolfer* alone," she stated again. "Finley is some help and he will awake soon, but we need Mahew. I don't know what is wrong with him."

"Cursing seems to take a lot from him," commented her cousin looking at the dried blood marks on her skin and clothes. "Could you not at least wash his blood off your face?" he asked pointedly.

She touched her features. "Was it a curse? You said the last one affected Lorland immediately."

"What else could it be?" asked Tranin taking a long sip of his tea. "You didn't see his face when he was standing over his dead."

"You didn't see his face when he confronted me on the street," she countered.

"And what did it look like, little cousin?" he queried with a cynical look in his eyes.

She shivered, "Okay, I was terrified of him, but still I want to hear it from his lips if it was a curse."

"He may not know," said Tranin handing her the mug. "Be careful, Minnow."

"We need them both," said the girl practically.

"I'm going to take another walk through what is left of the port."

"Can you do anything for his family?" she asked.

"I've already done what I can," said Tranin. "The ground will be too hard to dig, but I've put them out of reach of the scavengers. Go drink some of your own tea to warm up. You're shivering," he said as he headed back into the port with an empty sack.

"Get water," she countered.

* * *

CHAPTER 29

When Finley woke he looked at his surroundings. Then his face found Mahew's still form. Maru rose from where she had been sitting to lay a calming hand on the red-head's shoulder in passing.

She returned with a mug of hot sweetened tea. "Drink, Finley."

"How long?" asked the man between drinks.

"It is late morning. Tranin's crisscrossed the port and brought back anything useful. We're still here, because the two of us cannot manage the boat and keep an eye on both of you."

"I'm fine," replied Finley sitting up.

Maru pushed him back against the mattress. "Rest for now. There will be soup for lunch."

She looked at where Mahew lay, pale and gray. Only the occasional movement of his chest hinted that he breathed.

"You're covered in blood," commented Finley.

"Yes."

"Are you hurt? Did he hurt you!"

"What was he doing, Finley. Do you know? Could you tell? Was it a curse?"

Finley seemed to shrink back against the wall of the berth. "It was confused. He was angry...he was...he was mad...out his mind. I tried to stop him."

"I saw you. He knocked you down."

"No, I tried to stop what he was doing with his dream. It was twisted, and he was too strong. I couldn't stop him."

"You know what he did?" she asked intensely.

Finley shook his head slowly, "No."

"And what about Mahew now?" she asked. "What can we do for him?"

Finley looked at the silent man. "I don't know. He's never been this far gone before."

"Gone? Gone where?" Maru stared at the bluish face and felt out of her depth. "Can you bring him back from where he has gone?"

Finley shook his head. "I think he just needs time."

"Was it a curse, Finley?" she asked one more time.

He didn't answer her.

She smiled at him, "Sleep a little longer then. Later Tranin and I will need help. We want to leave as soon as possible, perhaps on the next tide."

"No, I'll go help him now," said the man getting to his feet cautiously and moving around her to get to the hatch.

He didn't want to be any closer to me than he needed to be, she thought. I'm asking all the questions he does not wish to answer. Or perhaps it was Mahew he was avoiding.

She brought the soup kettle up with bowls at mid-day. The men had been discussing options.

"How's Mahew doing?" asked Tranin. Finley kept his eyes on his food.

"I don't think anything has changed."

Tranin frowned. "On the ship he was out for half the watch." He turned to Finley, "What do you think?"

Finley shrugged.

Maru could see that irritated her cousin. "I'm going back down. I'll take the bowls with me." She left as quickly as she could. Nothing was going to be discussed in front of her that was clear.

She cleaned up the utensils, drank a mug of hot tea and felt the exhaustion of the last week sweep over her. She stuck her head out the hatch to tell the others, but the ship appeared to be empty. A fresh set of footprints were in the snow leading away from the ship.

She needed a few minutes rest she decided and laid down.

The dolfers were swimming in an ocean of blood. Maru reach out a hand to them and found she was swimming in the same ocean. It was everywhere.

Something touched her face. It was gentle and at first, she thought perhaps a wave had gently brushed her cheek.

She woke with a start to find Mahew's face bent over her. She flinched. His eyes were slightly out of focus. He held a damp cloth in his hand.

"You've hurt yourself," he said pulling back his hand.

"No," she said watching his eyes.

"But there's blood all over you." He leaned forward again and wiped at her face.

She took the cloth and finished the cleansing. "Do you remember what happened?" She shifted so she was not pinned in by him.

He sat next to her on the edge of her berth and frowned. He took several moments. "Striden," he said finally, "We're in Striden and they're all dead."

"Yes," said Maru softly. "I'm sorry."

Pain and anger crossed his features and for a long moment Maru was uncertain what he would do next.

"If you aren't hurt, why are you covered in blood?" He gently pushed aside a stray strand of her hair.

"Mahew, do you remember what happened after you found your family dead?"

He thought about her words carefully. "Brandt, I didn't find Brandt."

"I don't know. Tranin and Finley mentioned your sister and mate, but Finley would know what Brandt looks like, yes?"

"Yes," is was drawn out as his eyes narrowed. "Then she is not here." She could see the anger growing on his face and even she realized with surprise within him. The shaggy brown was darkening and solidifying into something impenetrable or inflexible, she wasn't sure what described it best.

"Mahew, no," she said softly.

He looked at her as if realizing she was present.

"Don't go there again, Mahew, please."

"What happened?" he asked, the edge of his anger was hinted at in his voice.

"I don't know exactly. You turned into a...thing. You know the legends of the sea, of the gleishens. I always thought they were to frighten children, but Mahew, you frightened me and now you don't even remember?"

He looked at the blood on her sweater. "I did this to you?" He seemed to notice the bandage on his hand. "I cursed *you*?"

"I don't know, Mahew," she said feeling rather faint. "You were babbling words I didn't understand in a language I didn't recognize. You might have cursed me and our son. You were so violent and rough that I don't know what else it could be." And that's what Finley and Tranin fear also, Maru realized.

"I wouldn't, couldn't curse you," he said. "Please, Maru, I couldn't." He shook his head. "No, you are all I have left."

"I understand, if your family is gone, your son will be important."

"No, that is...not only my son. You, Minnow, you've seduced me completely. I want no one else and...I want nothing bad to happen to...you."

Mare shivered slightly.

"Am I not making myself clear?" he said more intently. "I love you. If anything were to happen to you, it would be a curse upon me."

"Time will tell, I suppose," she said trying to give him a smile.

She could see the anger building again. "I would never..."

She laid her hand on his arm, "Mahew, please, let the anger go. I could not take your wrath a second time."

"I was wroth with you?"

"Perhaps I misspoke," she said softly fearing his anger being loosed in the confined space of the cabin. "You were wroth with the universe. All I know is I cannot stand against that fury. Please if you say you could not hurt me I will trust that. Please, let the anger go."

He paused then looked down at the floor. "You do not have the same feelings for me," he said quietly. "I suppose I should have realized that. I took you from one captive situation with Lorland to another with me. I seduced you. I left you and I didn't tell you where I was going. I didn't tell you my plans to bring you to Striden and got angry at you when you told me how you felt about it. I don't even know if you want our child. I hope you do, but I understand that might be too much to hope. Whatever happens Minnow, I will do my best to earn your love and trust. I would swear it in blood, but you seem averse to that now."

He looked up at her with a gentle smile to calm her fears, but in his eyes, she could see the gleishen moving restlessly. He pretended his rage was gone and she pretended that she believed it was, but it lurked in The Shark's eyes.

* * *

CHAPTER 30

Tranin and Finley came back with various things including several thick sweaters. Maru took one that fit her and went below. She washed away the last of the blood on her skin and pulled on the woolen sweater. The bloody cotton one she took back on deck and threw into the sea. It bobbed in the water but did not sink. She turned her back on it to find three sets of eyes watching her. She smiled, pretending she didn't know they were talking about her.

Damn, she was doing a lot of that today. She moved towards the men. Mahew face looked pale despite his tanned skin. Finley looked only marginally better.

"We missed the tide," she commented.

"We can catch the one after sunset," said Tranin.

"We need to leave now," said Mahew.

"Considering we would not be here, if some of us had our say," Tranin said with an eye on the other two men, "I think your votes should not count."

Mahew had the decency to look down.

"Sunset will do," said Maru feeling the tensions. "Did you take care of the dead?"

"Those Finley and I could find. There were not a lot. The rest of the village must have been taken as captives."

"Where is the nearest place they could take them?" asked Maru looking at Mahew. No pretending he did not know.

"The lesser quality they would sell off quickly at the mines," said Mahew. "The best they would save for the market in Astral."

"We need to figure out a way to get Brandt back," said Maru.

All three men's heads turned in her direction.

"I've experienced Lorland's hospitality. He's behind this and I say we go to help Brandt."

"Maru, have you forgotten your father still thinks you a slave or worse, dead. My father is still in prison for you. You carry a child and you are not safe while in pirate waters as The Silnik's..."

"Daughter," she finished for him. "I am deathly sick of that title. I did not earn it. I did not want it."

Mahew sighed, "I have to agree with Tranin. I thought you would be safe here, that I could protect you, but I ...We need to get you to your father."

Maru looked at Finley and waited for his response.

"Why do we go for Brandt?" he asked Maru seriously. "It has a low chance of success."

Maru looked at the water. "Lorland doesn't expect it. He expected you to consider yourself safe here. He now will expect you to head for the next safest place. Not the least safe place."

Finley nodded.

"Minnow, we do not have the resources and all we will do is end up handing you back to Lorland." Mahew said softly.

"Where was *The Silver Fish* headed after she out sailed the other ship?"

"The Far Isles."

"Where can we find more men?" asked Maru practically.

"Maru, if we sail as far as the Isles, we can take you to Grantoli first," commented Tranin.

"I don't think The Silnik will listen to four of us. Grantoli might help," she said slowly, "but we should meet up with your men first and then involve Grantoli."

She looked at the men. "The tide ebbs at sunset. Tranin, you need to get some rest." She looked at the other two. "It wouldn't hurt you two either. I'll stand watch."

Mahew lingered after the other two went below. "Minnow, I don't know what I did to you, to our child, but I promise I'll make it up to you." He started to unwrap the hand with the knife cut.

Maru stopped the action. "No more blood today, please, Mahew." He looked at her. She leaned forward and kissed him. "Get some rest. We'll find Brandt."

Maru sat on the starboard rail and stared at the placid harbor. Sunlight glinted off the water. Maru decided that Lorland had raided Striden before he had raided Mahew's Astral home. It was clear from the few bodies she had seen that they had been dead a while, although none of the men would discuss it with her.

Maru was willing to bet that Lorland had not sold Brandt. She looked at *The Laughing Dolfer*. Mahew said Lorland did not trust others with his possessions, which meant...Brandt had to have been on *The Moon* or *The Raven* when Lorland had boarded *The Silver Fish*. He had spent a lot of time not on *The Silver Fish*.

With Mahew's curse that Lorland was impotent around Maru, had he gone back to one of the other ships to regain his manhood? And had the others realized this, she wondered? Of course, at the time none of them had known Striden was destroyed.

Tranin was correct, she sighed, that they needed to get The Silnik involved, but Maru was also aware that her father would never let her leave Grantoli if they went there first. So how to get a message to him, but not actually sail into Grantoli? She thought about the timing. Then she smiled. Maybe she could manage it. Especially if she could keep the men feeling guilty and manipulate the duty roster so she was at the wheel at the correct time. Judging from how quietly they had just followed her orders it looked like she might be able to pull it off.

The timing was perfect she realized two weeks later. With favorable currents and winds the light *Dolfer* had made winning time covering distances that would take slower ships almost three weeks. Tonight, was the new moon. The men had wanted to sail to the south further west than she planned but she told them they would avoid the eyes of her father's warships ringing Grantoli by sailing past them at night therefore gaining the helping speed of the natural southern currents closer to Grantoli. She had manipulated the duties so that she had the helm. Mahew stayed up and talked with her for a while, but he had headed off for a berth an hour ago. Even the weather was co-operating. It was clear with a steady wind.

When she saw the first lights winking on the eastern horizon she knew she was close enough to the line of warships her father kept as a deterrent. Maru picked up a line and tied the wheel, so the ship would maintain a southern course, paralleling the barricade of ships, keeping them on her eastern horizon. She waited to make certain her work would hold. Once satisfied, she pulled out a lantern, a piece of punk, a flint and steel. With a spark she got the punk lit and then used that to light the wick of the oil lantern. She set the lantern on the port rail and adjusted the shutter over the window to open. She left it that way for about a minute and then began her message. She kept it to a few words. She repeated it four times and then snuffed out the wick. She replaced all the equipment, untied the wheel and then stowing the line where she had found it.

Now to hope the message was noticed and passed on to her father.

* * *

CHAPTER 31

Tranin had been the first up to relieve her duty with two mugs of hot, sweet tea. He looked rested. "How close did we sail to the Grantoli fleet?" he asked, handing her a mug and taking over the wheel.

"I could see their lights on the horizon," she answered truthfully.

"Mahew's cooking breakfast." He took a sip of his tea. "How do we explain him to your father?"

"With a child on the way, I think that explains itself"

"But a pirate."

"Is he still a pirate if the pirates kill his family and burn his home?" She sighed, "It is all semantics."

Her cousin looked at her, "I think you don't want to go to Grantoli, because you know your father will lock you away."

"There is that," she said with a smile and taking a deep drink of the tea. "Once a silnik, always a silnik. I would hate to not have the freedom."

Tranin nodded. "Too bad you're a woman."

"But my father is not the problem...or rather is only a minor problem, Tranin."

"Lorland."

She nodded. "The raid on Grantoli was audacious. I think Mahew probably suggested it, but Lorland was more than willing to try it. What would he try next?"

"Without Mahew's brains, it probably won't be clever."

"But it will be bloody," finished Maru. "If we are to attack Lorland, I will need a martial skill."

"Minnow, you got your Test. Isn't that enough to prove your worthiness."

"This has nothing to do with worthiness, Tranin. It will take every hand we have to fight Lorland. I'm not sure I have time to learn how to use a sword, but I used to practice archery."

Tranin nodded.

Maru smiled at him. "You're willing to go along with that because archers usually stay on the ship!"

"There is that. Also, if you can keep your balance on a yardarm you're a difficult target."

"When we get to Mahew's ship help me practice."

"Yes. Speaking of Mahew," said Tranin nodding towards the hatch. Mahew approached carrying two bowls, followed by Finley with another.

"It's not as good as Cookie's, but it will fill you up," said the man handing Maru a dish. He took the wheel as he handed Tranin the other.

"What did you decide?" he asked scanning the horizon.

"Maru wants to improve her archery," said Tranin between bites.

"You can't think that we are taking you with us when we go up against Lorland?" he said with a frown in her direction.

"You are not my father and even he had a hard time keeping me in my *place*," she said with a frown. "And you'll need every able-bodied sailor."

"Tranin, you tell her," said Mahew.

Tranin laughed. "You tell Silnik Maru, I tried."

"So how many men do you have?" she asked.

Mahew considered it as he looked south. "Free, probably fifty. Those that Lorland has captured and would fight if I can get to them another fifty. Those that owe me and hate Lorland," he paused in thought, "maybe fifty to a hundred more."

"Oh," said Maru. "And Lorland?"

"Probably two hundred fifty to start with," said Mahew. "Unless I can show strength to match his, those favorable to me will not try going against him. It is not propitious, Minnow."

"But you are a shark," she said with confidence, "and will have a plan. Something simple but effective like what you two did at Grantoli."

Finley spoke for the first time, "Let us see what we find at the Far Isles." He looked at Maru as he said it. Maru had the feeling the red-head knew what she had done on her watch.

At the end of the day they caught sight of *The Silver Fish's* sails.

Cookie gave Maru a huge hug, lifting her off her feet the moment she set foot on the deck. "I knew they didn't get you!"

"And what about the crew," she said seeing many familiar faces.

"Scratches," said the cook with a grin.

"Lorland?"

"He was on one of the other ships unfortunately."

"And Lorland's men?"

Cookie didn't look so genial, "They jumped, or we tossed them over the side. Their friends picked them up or the sharks dined." He gave an evil grin.

At that point Mahew came up and the cook gave the silnik a salute. Mahew returned it than took Maru's arm and gently steered her away. Cookie smiled at the action and went back to greeting the other two men.

"Do you wish to have my cabin to yourself?" he asked quietly.

"Now?" she said in amusement, "Now you want to sleep alone?"

"We haven't slept together for the last two and a part months, I thought perhaps,"

"You weren't there and there was hardly privacy when you were, and I was angry with your condescending attitude," she rejoined, "and no I would rather share the berth with you."

His smile was the antithesis of the shark, she thought as he nodded and excused himself to speak with the first mate.

"The two of you have resolved your differences?" asked Cookie as he handed her a mug of hot tea.

"So it would seem," she said yawning at her tiredness.

"Minnow, it was destined."

Maru felt a kick and put her hand to her stomach.

"What's wrong?" asked the big man. "You've gone pale."

Maru looked at him in surprise, "The baby kicked."

The cook took her mug. "Off to bed," he said pushing her in the direction of the silnik's cabin. "And a blessing on you and the child."

'Yes, please,' thought Maru.

* * *

CHAPTER 32

Maru spent the next two days practicing with others in the cleared space spanning the length of the ship below decks. She concentrated on keeping her balance and shooting as the ship rolled with the waves. Meanwhile she wondered if her message had even been seen and if so, had they sent it on to The Silnik or decided it was a hoax?

She tried to focus on her aim but found her thoughts straying more than once. Was Brandt surviving?

Back on his own ship Mahew was inclined to exclude her from the discussions. It was irritating, for as a silnik she was entitled to sit in on such talks. Mahew said he didn't want her status revealed to the crew at this time, the same reason he also had about not bandied about her real name and connections to The Silnik.

"They are your crew. Don't you trust them?"

"It just it not the time," he repeated.

"Cookie knows I'm pregnant."

"Well in another few weeks it will be noticeable," sighed Mahew.

"And you hope to have me cached somewhere," she said with a sharp look.

"I don't want to put you at further risk."

"Mahew, if you had cursed me, I do believe it would have happened by now."

"Sometimes these things take a while," he said evasively. "We should make certain nothing happens to you."

"So, the men know I'm sleeping with you, and Tranin and I are related, but I still am not good enough to sit in on your war counsels."

"There is no reasoning with you when you are like this," he said stomping off.

'I'm not the one who stomped off in a huff,' she thought.

Darkin, the second in command who was leading the training, took her seriously. She recognized him as the one who had been amused by her name when Tranin had called her Minnow. When he handed out leather armor he approached her with one in hand. "This was the smallest I could find, Minnow. Wear a sweater underneath and it should fit right," he said without further comment.

On the third day when Mahew was busy planning without her, she climbed the rigging with the other archers to test her footing on the yardarms. They lay at anchor and the sea was beautifully calm, so the conditions were hardly challenging. Darkin had set a target adrift on a small float. They took turns shooting at it. The men cheered for each hit a sailor made. She was happy to see that several of her fletches were buried in the target. Her aim was good, but if the weather or sea were rough, that would be a different situation.

She had nocked another arrow when the watch in the topsail cried out, "Sails!"

Maru looked up to see in which direction he pointed then turned to the horizon and could just see the top of a sail.

"Another," cried another voice, soon joined by others.

Maru searched the horizon and except for the island to their back, the sails made a ring around *The Silver Fish*. There would be no outrunning whoever was coming at them. Maru reached back to count how many arrows she had remaining. She saw others doing the same. Not enough if they had to fight.

Mahew and Tranin came running on deck. Finley's red-head could be seen

lingering in the shadows of the galley.

"What kind of craft? What flag do they fly? What color the sails?" cried Mahew

loudly. He raised a spy glass as even those on the yards and spars looked to answer

his questions.

"A dozen ships," answered the master archer. "Ships of the line I would say,

silnik. The smaller craft maybe there, but too far to make out. Sails are white."

"I see that too," Mahew answered back. He stood frowning.

Nothing would prevent a ship from changing the color of its sails. Lorland could

be sailing white.

"What flag?" Mahew asked as he searched the nearest ship.

"I cannot see," replied Darkin. "You, sailor," he hollered at a man on a higher

perch and known to have excellent eye sight. "What flag?"

"The Silnik's, I believe," said the man searching.

"Grantoli is what they fly," Darkin confirmed to the silnik.

Maru hoped, but still held her bow ready. Flags were easily changed.

"Cry out if you recognize any ship," cried Mahew to the crew in the tops as he

passed his spy glass to Tranin. Tranin drew a bead on the nearest vessel.

"Up anchor," ordered Mahew at a bellow.

The men around her quickly slung their bows over their heads and began to

loosen the sheets. Maru worked alongside them to unfurl the sails.

Tranin keep the glass on the approaching ships.

Maru lifted her eyes long enough to a quick glance and for all she could tell they

were her father's, but Lorland's *Raven* had been the ship of the line.

Men worked the capstan as others prepared rigging. If they tried to run, she did not know where Mahew hoped to squeeze through. Maru pulled for all she was worth on the ropes as did the men around her. Darkin was suddenly at her side. He looked at her work and nodded, then moved on to another sailor walking the yard arms as if on dry ground.

Tranin added his voice above the chaos, "Hold, I recognize *The Gull* and *The Venger*. They are Grantoli."

Tranin handed the spy glass back to Mahew. He strode to the side and looked then brought down the glass. "Belay the orders. We'll stand our ground. Do not bear arms. Darkin, have your men unstring."

"You heard the silnik, put up your bows."

Maru, watched Mahew and Tranin as she undid the bow string. She caught the bow through her sash. It was awkward but would stay. Then coiled the string and slipped it into her sash also.

She started retying the lines that a moment ago she had undone. Mahew and Tranin were arguing. She could not hear their words and their faces were calm enough, but she could see Finley looking rather ill and Cookie handing him a mug of what was probably tea.

The crew of *The Silver Fish* cleared the lines and dropped anchor quickly and quietly. They too were affected by the dynamics between her cousin and Mahew.

Father had sent the best of his top ships, decided Maru as she soon recognized five other vessels. One ship signaled that they wished to approach.

'Wished to approach,' thought Maru with a snort.

"Like we have a choice," said Mahew loud enough for the crew to hear. "Tell them we will parlay."

It was *The Gull* that approached. Not the newest or the biggest of the fleet, but still manned heavily as Maru noted the archers lining the spars and arms.

As they drew along-side a man at the rail called out. "Prepare to be boarded in the name of The Silnik."

It was hardly a request.

Mahew nodded graciously and answered, "Come aboard."

The ship shook slightly as a heavy boarding plank was dropped onto *The Silver Fish*. Even Maru winced at the wood and paint that would chip. Two sword bearing sailors crossed to take up positions on either side of the plank. Next Maru recognized Admiral Saysel. Maru looked down on the tableau below. She noticed that Tranin had faded back into the general mill of sailors.

"Welcome aboard Admiral Saysel," said Mahew loud enough to carry to both ships.

"Do I know you?" asked the man as an aide and two more sailors crossed the gangplank.

"I imagine I have not been brought to your notice. I've shipped into Grantoli a time or two and The Silnik's top sailor is known to all that sail the southern seas."

Saysel was only listening to Mahew in a distracted way. His eyes were scanning the crew.

"And how might I, and my crew, help you?" asked Mahew.

"We are looking for someone," said Saysel. His focus sharpened quickly as Tranin did not manage to turn his head away quite in time. "You, sailor!" he ordered.

Mahew looked around in surprise, "I could help you if I had a name," he said.

"That one," ordered Saysel to his men as Tranin tried to move back further in the crowd. With grace her cousin gave it up and came forward.

Two sailors took up positions on either side. Still Maru waited where she was.

"I know you," stated Saysel. "What is your name and clan?"

"Yes, you know me, Admiral. Tranin, my father is Traru. My clan Trawn."

Saysel nodded. "It's been a while since our paths have crossed, Tranin." His aide blanched and disappeared back over the gangplank. "And now you ship with pirates?"

"Merchants," corrected Mahew. "You may check the ports I've visited. *The Silver Fish* brings legal goods and asks fair value only."

"Then you will not mind if we search your vessel further?"

"Again, if you tell me what you are looking for, I could help you locate it."

At that moment there was a commotion among the ranks on *The Gull*.

It was The Silnik, Maru realized from her perch. Perhaps it was the sun glinting off the water on the far side of the other ship, but she would have sworn there were flames of lighting shooting from the ends of her father's blond hair. He marched fiercely forward as his crew fell back.

Tranin looked up in surprise as Saysel stepped back to bow and give place to The Silnik. The men of *The Silver Fish* all bowed in equal measures of respect and awe. Silnik Mertin did not pause until he came to stop in front of Tranin. And that was when Maru realized he had a dagger drawn on Tranin's neck.

"Where is she!" he demanded. "Where is Maru?"

Tranin's arms were pinned by two sailors and another one held Mahew off at the end of a sword.

Maru sighed and passed her arrows and bow to another sailor. Finding the nearest anchored line, she swung a leg around the rope and descended quickly, slowing just enough at the end to drop to the deck rather than crash into it. She picked herself up and found that the fourth sailor had his sword pointed her way.

"I believe you are looking for me," she said simply moving forward to stand between Mahew and Tranin.

Her father's knife clattered to the deck as he grabbed her into a hug that enfolded her completely. "Maru, where have you been, child?"

He held her out at the end of his arms and finally smiled. "You look just like your mother."

The words stirred murmurs on the ships. Maru noticed only the pain in her father's eyes.

"I never meant to hurt you, Father," she said.

The word 'father' was quickly echoed around and over both ships.

"And Tranin is not to blame for anything that has happened."

"Silnik Mertin, if you wish to use my cabin to talk with your daughter further, I am certain my cook can find you some refreshment, such as it is."

Maru could see the term 'silnik' morph her father back into that role. "That would be welcome. I will speak with you in a moment," he said at Tranin, then turned to include Mahew, "You also, silnik." The whole time he did not let up his hold of Maru.

Maru moved toward the cabin with her father firmly gripping her arm. "You will not slip so easily from my hold this time, daughter," he said.

Again, the word 'daughter' echoed from those closest to hear to reverberate around the deck as the door closed behind them.

He crushed her in his hug. "Maru, I cannot tell you what agonies you have put us through."

Maru let his hold envelope her. She could almost feel she were a small child again.

"Are you well?" he asked finally, holding her at arm's length to look at her. "Intare, I would not have recognized you except you do look the very double of your mother."

"Was mother ever this sunburnt?" asked Maru with a small laugh.

"Yes, and with the same glow that I don't recall seeing before."

"Then you will say that I've been well looked after," she said.

"Have you? Traru said *The Dolfer* was boarded by pirates, was it this scoundrel?"

"Father, there is a long story to tell and it might be best if the others involved are here to tell their parts."

"Who sent the message?" he asked with a lift of his eyebrow.

"I did," she admitted, "not because I was facing duress, but we need your help."

"*We* need my help," he said looking at his grown child.

"Silnik Mahew, needs your help."

"Mahew," said her father with a chill creeping into his voice. "That is a name I have heard often. And he can call himself a merchant?"

"He does sail merchandise, but he also was dealing with the pirates until they turned on him. It will make more sense if the others are here. Trust me on this."

There was a knock at the door. When Maru opened it, Cookie entered with a tray. He gave her a wink. "Refreshments, Silnik."

"Set them there and tell your silnik and Tranin I wish to see them."

"And Finley also," said Maru.

"Finley?" said her father. "Is there anyone else we should include?"

She shook her head and The Silnik waved the cook out. "What kind of sailor name is Finley?"

"I don't think it is. He comes along the Western Coast. He is a healer. Be gentle please."

"You have swum in strange waters, Maru."

"That is very true, Father."

"Speaking of which Traru said you even swam the Test and passed."

She nodded.

"But of course, his voice cannot count as testimony."

"There were two others if they were not killed when *The Dolfer* was taken," she said pouring her father a mug of tea.

"Traru would not give their names."

"I expect he wanted to shield them if I did not turn up," she said practically. "Parder and Welden."

"We'll find them and see what is said, but," he smiled at her as he sipped his tea, "I do not doubt Traru's word."

"So why did you throw him in prison?" she asked.

"You have good sources for not having been in Grantoli for many months."

"News is carried on the wind," she quoted a sailor proverb.

"As you might imagine, I was angry and rather than hang him, I threw him in prison. I did relent and would have set him free, but he would not hear of it. He seemed to prefer it. I think he was feeling guilty."

He took another sip of his tea. "Now what is there between you and this pirate silnik?"

* * *

CHAPTER 33

Maru was saved from answering as there was a crisp knock at the door.

"Enter," said The Silnik.

One of her father's sailors opened the door.

"Send them in," said her father, "You may wait outside."

"Silnik..."

"Outside."

Mahew led the way with his disinterested shark's smile. Tranin looked more guarded. Finley looked faint.

The Silnik poured tea and passed mugs around.

"I have a bottle of something stronger," suggested Mahew moving closer to Maru.

"Maybe later," said Mertin. He looked at Finley as he handed the man a mug. "Will you be okay?"

Finley nodded.

Mertin looked at each in turn. "My daughter says I need to hear the whole story and that it requires all of you to tell it. I take it this will require time, so sit."

"From Traru, I have the story up to the point where *The Laughing Dolfer* was boarded," The Silnik said as he seated himself and got comfortable. "Where he had told you to take care of my daughter." He looked at Tranin.

Her cousin shifted in his seat.

"Your father is well," anticipated Mertin.

"I understood him to be imprisoned."

"He insisted and the guest rooms at the crest of Palace Mount," said Mertin. "are hardly strenuous."

"It depends on your freedom," said the younger man.

"We can discuss that later. I want to know what has happened for the last three months and why my daughter is just now brought back to my care?"

Maru started to open her mouth but closed it without saying anything.

"So where do we start?" asked The Silnik sitting back and drinking his tea.

Mostly the time went smoothly with The Silnik interrupting only to clarify a point or two. Maru could tell when her father was upset as Finley's features would grow paler. The others also noticed and choose their words with more care.

"And why was it you chose Maru as your portion of the booty?" he asked again.

Finally, Mahew said, "Would you believe me if I said I was worried some asshole would beat her into submission?"

"No."

Mahew shrugged. "She was the best piece he had, and he owed me more."

"And then you raped her?"

"Silnik Mertin, I am friends with Finley who you may have noticed is extremely affected by the people around him. If I were the type of person you are suggesting, Finley would never have stayed my comrade. You may also ask your daughter what happened."

Maru felt herself blush.

The Silnik studied her reaction and turned back to Mahew. "So, what did happen?"

"We enjoyed each other as men and women are meant to do," he answered.

Maru felt even warmer.

"Of course, it didn't hurt that you had blackmailed each of us into cooperating," commented Tranin offhandedly.

"Maru?" asked her father.

"Mahew did extract a promise, but there was no further pressure."

"After my fruitless trip to Grantoli to speak with you..."

"And you came to Grantoli to ..." interrupted The Silnik.

"Find out what I could about Traru and to offer information on the pirates," said Mahew.

"Not to bargain over the release of my daughter?"

"I still thought her your niece."

"Hmm."

Finley shifted where he sat.

"Since I did not speak with you, I returned to Astral only to realize my position with Lorland was more precarious than I had realized, and I made plans to remove Maru to a place I thought would be safer. I did not want Lorland to know, so I sent two sailors to wrap her up in a rug and carry her back to *The Silver Fish*."

"So why such concern for a fruit?" said her father.

"I do not think of her that way."

"So, you slept with him on the ship?" asked The Silnik looking at his daughter.

"No," she said blushing.

"She slept in the cook's supply room," answered Mahew.

The Silnik looked at him questioningly.

"We had a fight and,"

"You gave her to the cook? So that's what you thought of her?"

"She wanted to be…helpful…to have a purpose. I told the cook she was his scullery help, nothing more."

"You had my daughter scrubbing pots!" asked The Silnik incredulously.

"And decks every morning," added Mahew with all seriousness. "Perhaps she never angered you with her insistence that she needed useful work."

"Hmm," said The Silnik looking at his daughter.

"It was better than sitting staring at walls," said Maru. "I was useful."

"Until the morning Intare broke loose," sighed Mahew. "I was confident that Lorland would not follow us as he did not have any ships capable of catching us. I did not realize that I had left him the means when I left *The Moon* at Astral. Maru had hurt herself. Finley was healing her when Lorland's approach was noticed. In those few moments several things changed."

"Changed how?"

"I told him Maru's true parentage," said Tranin.

"Why then?" asked The Silnik.

"Because with Lorland approaching I needed all the help I could find to protect her," admitted her cousin. "Mahew may have been angry with my cousin at times, but he was never malicious."

"What else changed?"

Finley finally spoke, "As I healed Maru's burns I was aware that she was with child and I told Mahew."

There was a solid silence. The Silnik looked at Finley as if he had not heard correctly. He looked Mahew and then Maru. "You are pregnant?"

Maru nodded.

"Your child?" he said to Mahew.

"Our child," said the man

"Our son," corrected Maru.

Her father looked at her and nodded. "I told you that you looked like your mother. Now I remember exactly when." He looked at Mahew, "I am still not letting my daughter be mates with a pirate."

"I think you don't have a say, Father," said Maru gently.

There was a second silence.

Mahew broke the tension. "At that moment there was no time for considerations except to keep Lorland from slitting Maru's throat."

Tranin nodded. "So, we gave Lorland the ship and were thrown in the brig."

"And Maru?" asked Silnik Mertin.

"Lorland took me for his," said Maru softly.

Her father's face darkened with anger. Finley's paled in equal measure.

"And Mahew laid a curse that I would wish on no man," said Tranin with a smirk.

Mertin looked at his nephew and the pirate then his daughter. "How did you fare with Lorland?"

"He tried," said Maru, "But gave up in anger." She decided the beating was not relevant.

"So, at this point, Lorland had my daughter and your ship?"

"It was still *my* ship," corrected Mahew. "We just needed the right moment to retake it."

"We used *The Dolfer* to escape while my men fought Lorland's. We sailed for my home port. I still had the idea I could safely leave Maru there and now that I knew she was pregnant I was determined on that course. But," sighed Mahew, "I didn't realize Lorland had been there before us."

"The port was destroyed," said Tranin when the other man did not continue. "Lorland had been there at least a month before. The dead we found or what was left of them were the babes or the ancient. We...we were all stunned."

"And," said Maru, "Mahew lost his remaining family. His sister and husband were among the dead and his niece among the missing."

Mahew's face was stony.

Finley was looking faint.

"We all decided that the best plan was to get help," continued Tranin.

"So why bypass Grantoli?" asked The Silnik.

"We did not know what reason to give you to elicit your help," said Tranin.

"I did not want to be locked away," added Maru. "We agreed to rendezvous with Mahew's ship and decide."

"But you sent me a message anyway," said her Father.

The other three men stared at her, realization dawning on their faces to be verbalized by Tranin. "Of course, the night we would have sailed past the fleet you were at the helm."

"We need your help, Father," she answered calmly, "I just need it not to be on your terms."

"But it still appears that it will be on my terms," said The Silnik looking at each of them in turn. "A pirate, a traitor to his kin, a wayward daughter and ..." he paused looking at Finley, "Well, you I could forgive as you seem to have been pulled along with the happenstances."

"Silnik," said Mahew rising from his seat, "I will gladly swear allegiance to you or face whatever punishment you deem suitable, but I kept Maru from that man not because she was your daughter, but because I love her. I also need to find my niece and I ask your help in dealing with that monster." He had pulled his knife from his sash and before anyone could react he had cut his hand and dripped blood on the table. "I swear, I am your bound servant, Silnik Mertin."

Maru watched the blood as it fell. Three evenly timed drops of scarlet. The first one splashed onto the table top. The second added itself to the first enlarging the stain.   The third bloated the spot to spatter outward running across the table, spilling onto the floor and filling the cabin. It poured out the windows and doors. Maru flailed as she found herself drowning in a red sea. She heard a noise and looked overhead to see dark wings swooping towards her. Claws reached for her and she screamed raising her arms to futilely ward off the danger.

* * *

CHAPTER 34

As she gained consciousness Maru was aware of several things. It was night and the ship was no longer at anchor. Judging by the rise and fall they were fully underway. When she opened her eyes, she realized she was no longer on Mahew's ship. This was not his cabin.

She felt woozy and unsettled.

"Here, drink this."

Maru turned to find Finley sitting near the head of the berth she was in, his face lit by the low light of a brazier. He offered her a mug of water.

She sat up slowly and drank cautiously.

"Feeling better?" he asked.

She smiled at him, "I don't know why you ask when you know."

"Convention," he answered with a smile. "People don't expect me to really know what they are thinking or how they are feeling."

"Why are we not on Mahew's ship and where are Tranin and Mahew? Father didn't throw them in irons, did he?"

"Mahew thought you would be safest with your father and your father naturally agreed," said the man with a smile. "Tranin has gone ahead to scout with *The Laughing Dolfer.*"

"To scout?" she asked. "For what?"

Finley looked at her closely, "What was the last thing you remember, Maru?"

She looked around for the blood that had saturated her last thoughts. "Mahew made a blood vow and the drops..." she frowned.

"The drops," prompted Finley taking the mug from her.

"They filled the ocean. I was drowning in them and the shadow wings were diving for me."

"Nothing more?" he questioned gently.

"No. What happened?"

Finley went and refilled her mug, but this time from a teapot on the brazier. He handed it to her and waited until she had taken a good drink. "Mahew called it 'riding the waves'. He said you had done it before."

"I know the term," she answered. "To foresee the future, but I've never done it."

"Mahew says you have."

"When?" she asked. She took another drink, frowning at recalling any such event.

"He said he made a blood vow in your presence once before and you went into a trance."

Maru paled, "In Astral, I fainted."

"You did not faint. What you said then was to warn Mahew of Lorland. He did not entirely believe your words. A thing he has come to regret." Finley looked at her thoughtfully. "A reason he is concerned that perhaps he cursed you in Astral."

"And what did I say this time?"

"First let us consider that Lorland would like to destroy our silnik. Where did he strike Mahew first?"

"His family's homeport," said Maru. "And then his house and ships in Astral."

Finley nodded. "So where does that leave Mahew to go. Unlike others that sail the southern seas, Mahew under another name, has also free access to..."

"Grantoli," said Maru spilling the drink before Finley could take it from her. "Intare, would he dare?"

"Lorland has already sailed in and out of there once. Who would expect him to do so again and so soon after the last raid?"

"We have to warn them," said Maru trying to throw aside the blanket over her.

"Your father sent messenger pigeons and we are underway as quickly as his fleet can travel. Tranin is scouting ahead."

"And Mahew?"

"Well, your father was doubly stunned by Mahew's vow and by your reaction to it. It appears the two of you have an unusual link in abilities. When Mahew makes a vow or a curse it will be fulfilled, and you apparently see what others do not. Together I think you might change futures. I do not think there will be any further discussion of his being unsuitable for you."

"You don't know my father," sighed Maru. "What did he do with Mahew?"

"Mahew is silnik still of *The Silver Fish*. The plan is to arrive at Grantoli's harbor at morning."

"Will we be in time?"

"That will depend on what Tranin finds."

There was a knock and the door opened. Maru saw her father in the low light. "May I enter?"

"Certainly Silnik," said Finley taking Maru's mug and setting it on the table. "Maru is feeling better. Let me know when you are finished."

"Is he my guard now?" she asked her father.

"Only of his own choice," said the man finding a mug and filling it with the contents of the teapot. "You keep surprising me, Maru. I would have locked you away in the palace on Grantoli, and I admit it would have been a mistake."

"You would have done it only because you thought that would protect me."

"Well, one wants to shelter their children as you will learn. I said earlier that you have become very like your mother. I just had not realized that it was in more than just the physical appearance." He stared as small tongues of flame licked the bottom of the teapot. "You were so young when she died. I imagine you don't remember her that well."

"You never spoke of her," Maru said hearing the accusation in her voice.

"No, I did not. It was too painful to remember how brilliant a soul she had been and then see her pale and cold as they wrapped the shroud around her dead body. I never understood why she died.

"I think I would have allowed myself to die if I hadn't had a small daughter to consider." He looked at her and took a sip of his tea. "Even so, I think I only came out of that depression when I met Jasmin. I was no comfort to you and for that I am sorry." He shook his head. "I missed what you have become. You are an independent soul as your mother was and you must follow your own course. I would wish you to be safe, but I can hardly guarantee that you are."

He set down the mug, "He has skirted the law and perhaps come down on the correct side of the line this time, Maru. I do not know if he will always do so." He looked at her in the faint light that was finding its way in through the windows.

She did not need him to name Mahew. "I think, that Finley as his friend says he will," the young woman.

"That he cares for you gives me more hope," said her father. He looked at the leather armor she still wore from the previous day.

"So, Maru, I imagine I would have to tie you to something to keep you out of the coming fight."

"Yes, Father."

"Then I guess you better find a bow, a quiver of arrows and take your place in the tops."

She stood to face him.

"I would ask you not to wear your red sash, Maru. There will be enough silniks to make targets for Lorland's men. I would ask you, not tell you."

She nodded.

He gave her a crushing hug. "You do your mother proud."

* * *

CHAPTER 35

Maru heard the lookout's shout that indicated the scouting party was spotted. Mertin had his men drop sail and sent a signal to the other silniks to convene on *The Gull*. Maru pulled the sash from where she had folded it under her armor and tied it at her waist. She waited quietly as the other silniks arrived   Mahew found her and joined her to one side of the group. Neither of them were certain of their reception with The Silnik's conclave, but for differing reasons.

"I see he let you have a bow and arrows," commented Mahew.

"I promised to be cautious," she said.

Mahew snorted.

Mertin held the conclave on the open deck of *The Gull*. Maru and Mahew stood to the outer edge of the gathering. Her father gave her a nod of recognition but made no public acknowledgement. In the lightening sky her shape would be just another silnik's.

Tranin's report gave Lorland's fleet closing on Grantoli sooner than The Silnik's.

Among the silniks that had sailed with Mertin the longest there was grumbling that they should never have left Grantoli so lightly defended. Her father heard them all and did not disagree or defend his decisions.

"What is done, is done," he said. "What we need is the plan for today. Lorland will easily over power the few ships that remain. He will head straight for the port. We bottle him up inside the harbor."

"We will not have the ability to maneuver in the harbor," said someone. Admiral Saysel, Maru thought.

"And neither will he," replied her father. "If we can foul their lines the smaller craft in port will be able to cut and slash at them while they are dealing with us."

Murmurings arose as the silniks discussed the tactics.

"It's the best of a bad deal," said an old silnik. "He will be just as handicapped as we, but the smaller craft should tip the balance in our favor."

The silniks found their oarsmen and made for their ships.

Mahew pulled Maru into a dark corner and kissed her. "Be careful, Seafoam."

"May I ask you to do the same?" she answered.

Mahew looked her in the eye and nodded.

They kissed once more then Maru headed for the rigging. From the first yardarm she watched in the early light as Mahew made his way back to *The Silver Fish*. She took her sash off, folded it and slipped it back under her armor. The anchor lines that had temporarily held *The Gull* back were raised. Maru felt the breeze strengthen as they got underway. She helped with the rigging when possible.

They were sailing directly into the sun. Maru concentrated on keeping her footing. This was much rougher than the little practice she had at The Far Isles. If anyone on Lorland's armada looked back the Grantoli fleet would be easily seen in the morning light. Her father ordered all the sail the ship was possible of setting. *The Gull* moved slightly ahead of the other ships. Mahew's ship kept pace on the starboard side. Tranin had *The Dolfer* out ahead.

The headlands on either side of the harbor entrance had curls of smoke rising from them. The attack was on. Mertin did not slacken *The Gull's* speed and they shot between the guard towers and the two ships harassing them. Others would deal with them.

Maru joined the men among the rigging in stringing her bow and checking her arrows. To her right Mahew's ship showed no sign of slowing. She could see his red sash as he gave orders. Ahead sailed Lorland's ships. Maru searched for a ship she might recognize and then saw the pirate's *Raven*, towards the back of the fleet. Trust Lorland to not lead from the front, though Maru readying an arrow.

"*The Raven* is there," she cried as loudly as she could. "That is the pirate's flagship."

Heads turned in her direction. The Silnik looked to her position then turned his spy glass in the direction she indicated. Mahew's men were already familiar and needed no help from Maru to find their target. Already *the Silver Fish* was ahead on her altered course.

Maru could not hear her father's words, but *The Gull* swung in the direction she had indicated. Behind them the other ships of the line fanned out to encircle the pirate fleet, but *The Gull* and *The Silver Fish* sliced right for the heart. Lorland's ship would be sandwiched between them. Mahew was not taking any care about contact as he approached. Maru braced herself in the rigging and prepared to fire.

She heard the impact as Mahew slammed *The Silver Fish* into the starboard side of *The Raven*. In the moment before the blow a hail of arrows had rained down on the pirates to be answered with return volleys. *The Gull* was still just out of range of the archers. Maru watched as grappling hooks were flung from *The Fish* and ready men swung across the short distance.

"Caution," she muttered under breath as she watched the scarlet sash move among his men.

Then she was too busy as the master archer of *The Gull* gave the call for his men to fire. Maru's arrows could not cover the same distance as the others, so she picked her targets the best she could. She had no time to keep track of Mahew.

"Brace" shouted several voices.

She had enough time to grab a line as she lost her footing in the jarring, grinding contact *The Gull* made with the pirate vessel. She pulled herself back on the yard arm in time to see Lorland send a man below.

Maru took only a moment to make her decision as she sent another arrow into a pirate's thigh. It was not a killing shot, but another sailor finished him with a sword. Lorland was loath to leave his prizes, such as *The Laughing Dolfer*, behind that meant Brandt was likely to be on *The Raven*.

The broadside hit that Mahew had given the ship had to have loosened some of the caulking. The ship might even now be taking on water and if Maru was right...

She slung her bow around her shoulders and looked for a line that would carry her over to the pirate vessel. Others had already crossed from *The Gull* and *The Fish* to fight hand to hand. Maru found a line and taking a deep breath jumped into the void of air.

She fell a distance before the rope stretched out and swung her in the direction she wanted. Several feet above *The Raven's* deck she let go and dropped on top of two men who had been wrestling each other for the control of a knife. One grunted and went limp. The other came up with the bloody knife and looked at her. Maru lost no time jumping to her feet and fleeing in the direction that would lead her to the holding cell she had known when last, she had been on Lorland's ship.

No one followed her. The noise of battle overhead was muted but echoed in the empty spaces below deck. It was dark and only two lanterns gave any light compared to the morning light above.

Maru oriented herself and started for where she remembered the cell being. Looking ahead she saw two guards arguing outside the area. She pulled three arrows to hold and nocked one. Calming her breathing let the barb fly. One man went down face first. The second looked her way in time to catch the second arrow in his arm. He started running down the space between them with sword drawn. Maru tried not to tremble as she fitted the third arrow quickly and fired it. He fell a foot from her position. Stepping around him she hurried to the cell.

Huddled against the far corner were five women. Maru located the keys on the hook that had so tantalized her the last time she had been here. She opened the cell door.

"Come on," she said waving at the cowering mass.

"Minnow?" asked the woman facing her.

"Hello, Darlow," she said. "Get them out of here. The Silnik's ship is on the port and Silnik Mahew's is on the starboard. Get to either one and you should find safety."

"Mahew, you said Mahew," said a brown-haired girl as she stumbled forward. "Mahew, Bacher Mahew?"

"I only know him as Mahew," said Maru pulling another woman from the cell.

"From Striden," asked the girl.

"Are you Brandt?" Maru asked her own question.

"Yes," sobbed the girl.

"Then get on your uncle's ship and take the others with you."

Maru led the way back to the upper deck. At the top of the stairs she fired arrows point blank to clear a path for the women. At the rail of the ship she realized that *The Silver Fish* had received more punishment in the original collision and appeared to be taking on water quickly.

"Intare," she cursed. There was no guaranteed relief in that direction. She indicated they should follow her as she led the way aft. Then she saw a welcome sight. *The Dolfer* was just astern of the pirate ship.

Maru waved as large as she could to get Tranin's attention. Just another sailor from his position, she decided. She found her sash and pulled its scarlet silk out to wave in the air. She got a responding wave back. She stuffed it back inside the vest.

Maru found a coil of line and tied knots as fast as she could to secure it to the ship. "Climb down," she said tersely as she watched back towards the main deck and the heat of the fighting. "*The Dolfer* will get you."

The women looked at her dubiously until Darlow took over. "Grab the rope and slide down. That or climb back into Lorland's berth."

"And you?" Darlow asked as she sent the last woman over the rail.

"I've got a curse to fulfill."

Darlow gave her an evil grin then disappeared over the rail.

Maru leaned over to check how the women fared and just heard the whistle of something flying past her head. She ducked and turned around.

* * *

CHAPTER 36

The sailor swung his sword at her again and Maru jumped to the side pulling her knife free of her sash. He slid the same direction she had jumped. He had her pinned against the rail and by his grin he knew it. Now he was toying with her as he faked a lunge and watched her jump.

With it slung over her back her bow was useless even as a weapon to poke or thrust. The next lunge was not faked, and Maru skipped aside just barely. While the sailor's moment took him forward she tried for ducking under his weapon. Her bow caught on his arm and knocked her to the deck on her back looking up at the man grinning down at her. Using her knife, she slashed at the back of his ankle. He howled and hopped on one foot, hacking at her. She rolled to the side just in time, got to her knees and turned to face him with the ship to her back. He had his weight on his good leg.

He leapt at her and she jumped back but tripped over a coiled line and landed on her rump. She heard and felt the bow crack beneath her. She brought the knife up to ward him off. An arrow flitted past and planted in his shoulder. He stumbled back and went over the rail.

She needed a weapon and the pirate had been inconsiderate enough to take his sword with him. She tossed the pieces of the bow over the side when a hand fell on her shoulder. She tried to twist away but the hand held.

"Come, Minnow."

She found Parder had her firmly in his grip. "Your father wants you back on *The Gull.*" "He's willing to overlook our helping Traru if we get you back in one piece." Welden was keeping look out.

Maru nodded tucking her knife back in her sash. She looked to see where Mahew was. He was hurrying men off his ship and it didn't take much to see why. *The Silver Fish* was listing badly and would not stay above water much longer.

Parder was dragging her forward. Welden was opening a path for them until he was tied up with a sailor that would not yield easily. She and Parder slipped past. Swords clashed and clanged while men grunted and yelled in tight combat. Behind them there was a groan and gargle of sucking water. Maru looked back to see the tops of Mahew's ship sink into the water. Lines connected to *The Raven* stretched and a few snapped. Sailors closest stopped fighting to cut the remaining lines to the drowned ship.

Someone grabbed her braid and jerked her backwards hard. She fell against the man and found a large blade at her throat.

"Hello, Minnow," was hotly spoken into her ear. His stench was rank in her nostrils.

Maru looked for Parder and Welden. Both men were busy fighting for their lives. From the corner of her eye she saw a red sash. Mahew slashed at a man clearing a route towards where she was held by Lorland.

"Stand your ground, Mahew!" shouted Lorland.

Mahew stopped. Maru could see his lips moving and his features stiffen. She worried at what he would do.

Maru held onto Lorland's knife arm tightly with her right hand.

Lorland jerked her hair again pulling her neck away from the knife. With her left hand she felt for the knife she had used earlier. From the other direction she could see her father on *The Gull* with ten archers, arrows aimed their way waiting.

"This is not going to work, Lorland," she said cautiously. She found the knife hilt in her sash.

She could see Lorland's attention shift to take in The Silnik's ship.

"And why not, Minnow?" he breathed in her ear with a chuckle.

Mahew took a step forward when he thought Lorland was not looking. The knife nicked her throat as Lorland turned again towards the silnik.

"Because if I die, not only will Mahew kill you but you can count on The Silnik trying to beat him to the job."

"And why would that be?"

She could feel each time he shifted to keep an eye on the two men.

"Because he is my father."

"The Silnik," he laughed. "Better, Minnow. That increases my chances."

"But I'm going to change your odds," she said. "You will have to kill me and then you are a dead man."

He laughed in her ear.

She bit down on his knife arm with all her strength while burying her knife in his thigh as deeply as she could.

Lorland screamed. He pulled reflexively on her hair pulling her head in that direction even as the knife arm jerked away as her teeth kept their grip. Her mouth filled with taste of the sweat of his skin and his blood. He flung her away. She landed heavily skidding a foot or two along the deck to fetch up against a coil of line.

Mahew's shape shot past her as a blur while a swarm of arrows flew from *The Gull* and buried in Lorland's back.   Mahew knocked the captain to the deck throttling Lorland's neck with his hands and hammering the pirate's head repeatedly against the boards. The gleishen look was upon his face.

Maru crawled towards Mahew and reached out to touch his foot. "He's dead, Mahew. Let it go. Mahew." She tried to call his name more forcefully, but he paid her no heed.

"Bacher," she said softly. He paused at that and let Lorland's body drop one final time to the deck. He turned to stare at her. The look in his eyes was still wild and his features had much in common with the bear, bacher, now that she had thought about it. He moved to her side and touched the blood at her neck. The wildness faded. He pulled his sash off to press against her neck.

"That was stupid, Minnow."

"Not with your blessing protecting me, love," she whispered.

"Finley," he shouted above the fighting that had resumed around them. The Silnik's men cleared a path to their position. Cookie appeared followed by Finley who knelt beside her and took the sash away to look at the cut on her neck

"Take care of her," said Mahew rising.

Finley reapplied the sash and nodded at the silnik. Cookie's arms picked her up carrying her towards *The Gull*.

"Mahew," she cried out. It came out rather gargled.

The Raven shifted slightly tilting in the same direction *The Silver Fish* had disappeared.

"Mahew," she tried again as they passed her over the rail to *The Gull*. He waved her way and continued towards the entrance to the lower decks.

"She's not there," shouted Maru trying to get out of the arms of those who set her on the deck. She was promptly pushed back to the deck's boards.

Mahew turned at that.

"She's with Tranin on *The Dolfer*," she said. One of the men passed the message along as Maru found her voice too feeble. Mahew grinned and changed course as *The Raven* tilted more.

"What?" she asked feebly.

"He's going to get the rest of the men off the ship," said Cookie as Finley pressed his fingers against her neck.

"Relax, this will not take much."

"Cookie, Finley, call him back."

"Mahew will do as he wills," said the healer. "You'll have a scar." As soon as Finley removed his hand she scrambled to her feet.

She wavered and then took a breath. "Mahew," she shouted at the top of her lungs. She could not spot him.

Finley pulled her back from the rail.

"Well, Maru," she turned to face her father. "I should have known archery would not be enough." He looked her over carefully. "A worthy daughter."

There was a groaning of wood followed by splintering. Maru turned looking for Mahew. His sash was still in Finley's grip. She lunged for the rail.

"Mahew," she yelled watching the imploding ship sink beneath the waves. Men chopped at lines to free *The Gull*. "No," she cried as she spotted the silnik on the far side of the deck. He was staggering towards her position trying to keep his footing on the slanting top deck. His foot stepped into a coil of line. It was connected to an anchor that was sliding across the boards. The loop tightened, snagging Mahew's foot. He bent to try and free his foot as the anchor went over the far side slamming him to the deck. His hands scrambled to find a hold. They found nothing permanent. He gave that up as he returned at the last second to trying to free his foot again. He disappeared over the far rail.

Maru was almost over *The Gull's* rail before someone caught her and pulled her back. "Mahew!" she shouted again as *The Raven* sank beneath the waves taking Mahew with it. "No," she shouted at the universe, "NO!" She almost pulled free of the person holding her.

"You cannot go, Maru," said her father's voice in her ear.

She felt as if she were suffocating. She gasped for breath and still could not get any air. Her head grew light and her sight dim. Someone held her.

"Maru? Help her." It was her father's voice, but it sounded very distant.

"She is feeling Mahew's death. If she is not convinced to stay she will follow him." Finley's voice faded.

She felt the same cold envelope her as on the day of The Test.

"I am sorry daughter, but you cannot go after him, no more than I could follow your mother. He is gone, but you carry his child. A part of him will still live if the child lives." Slowly she could feel her father's arms. They held her tightly as tightly as she wished to hold Mahew. "Maru, you cannot go with him. You have your child to bear, to raise."

She heard him but wished she could not. The child within gave a fluttery kick bringing her back to the warmth of the sun and her father's arms.

"Mahew," she mumbled and felt the tears fall. Salty like the sea. "Mahew!" she wailed feeling the warm sunshine on her head as she screamed into her father's chest. She would be able to do what was needed, but it would cost a world of hurt.

"Take her to my cabin." She was numb as he passed her to another. Dully she recognized it was Cookie that led her away from the churning debris laden water.

* * *

CHAPTER 37

Maru stumbled along in Cookie's hold. She shut her eyes letting the other man lead her. Her feet faltered but the cook held her upright.

"Dolfers!" The cry changed the feel on *The Gull*. There was an eagerness. Maru opened her eyes to see all the eyes around her turned back in the direction she had just come. The faces were excited, and many sailors were pointing. Maru did not care to see the dolfers. Perhaps never again did she wish to see the sea. The cook had stopped but Maru shrugged off his hold and continued, wrapping her arms around herself to stop the deathly chill she felt. Others hurried past her to see the animals.

Her father was correct. She needed to raise a son. Another Bacher, a bear too stubborn to know he wasn't a sea creature.

"Look, look," cried a man on a spar. "They have something." A murmur of anticipation moved through the sailors.

It would be Mahew's body. How she knew, she was not certain, but that she could not abide to see it cold and dead was definite. She lurched on.

Dazedly she looked past the ship. All around ships were scattered. Many were broken and burning. Beyond lay the port and city of Grantoli. The afternoon sun shone brightly on the castle mount where the flags stood out in the breeze. She stared at the flags. Around her the babble rose. "It's Silnik Mahew." "Get him on board." "Watch it, you almost dropped him."

"Maru!" she heard Finley holler, but she ignored him and headed for her father's cabin. She needed to cocoon herself from the pain.

"Maru," said Parder grabbing her arm.

She tried to shake off the man's hold.

"Silnik Maru, Finley says Silnik Mahew is alive."

She stared at the sailor trying to make sense of his words. He had been underwater too long. She had felt him die. Was she wrong? A small hope started growing in her cold chest. "Alive?"

"Yes, silnik. Come," he said pulling her back to the rail where Cookie stood guard over a kneeling Finley and a still body. Mahew's red sash of authority lay as a wet lump and the only color except for an ugly bruise around Mahew's left ankle.

Maru felt lightheaded again and tripped in her hurry. Parder's hold kept her upright. She shook him off and stared at the man she loved.

Mahew's wet hair was slicked back against his skull and his kilt was plastered against his legs. She looked at the hair and noticed for the first time that it wasn't really a sailor blonde. Wet with water it glistened silver with no hint of gold. Her hair, even severely bleached by the sun, had a cast of yellow. His hair hadn't been blonde she thought. It was...she wasn't sure if she remembered the girl, Brandt, his niece and her brown hair. His hair wasn't brown either. It was colorless, like some albino creatures, but his skin wasn't white. Finley had white skin that never tanned. Mahew's had been a dark tan although his tan now was bluer than brown.

She looked at the color of his skin. Darker than most sailor bronzes. What was he or had he been if not sailor kind? And it appeared it would not matter, except she realized as the child within fluttered and reminded her he was there.

Maru stared at Mahew and saw no indication of life. No movement of the chest that would indicate inspiration of air. Finley's face had a vacant look and he did not appear to contain anymore life than Mahew.

The woman's hope was crushed again. She fell to her knees; her sobs the only sound. She took the wet sash and straightened it in her hands. She went to smooth its folds at his waist as was fitting for a dead silnik. The fingers of her right hand unexpectedly touched the skin above his kilt. She felt a snap of electricity as one did on dry winter days between metals and wool. She jerked her hand back.

Finley's head turned in her direction and he stared at her. He pulled his hands from where they rested on Mahew's neck and chest. Maru looked at the red-head's face. It was gray and drawn.

"Of course," said the healer in a soft voice, "of course."

"It is too late, Finley. He is dead."

"No," said Finley more firmly, "but I am not the right caller. You, Maru. You can call him back."

He took her hands and placed them where his had been a moment earlier. Maru felt as if a hive of bees buzzed between her hands and Mahew's cold skin. She would have pulled them away, but Finley held them firmly. There was a small movement of Mahew's chest that stopped her tears.

"Just call him, Maru. Do not use your energy, I'll provide that, but call Mahew to return."

For a moment she was content to follow the healer directions. But as Maru sensed what Finley was doing she decided to ignore his injunction.

'Maru, this is not wise,' she heard in her head.

'With him or not at all,' she thought shutting her eyes looking for that calm of which Finley seemed to have endless oceans. She tried to judge how much of her energy she could safely pass to the healer as she called, "Mahew!" into the void. "Mahew, we need you!"

Out of the gray that seemed to surround her she could make out a brown shape at a distance. It seemed to hesitate, then slowly turn.

"Mahew, please," she cast towards him. The brown head swung from side to side as if seeking.

"I love you, Mahew."

The shape stilled, then with a leap it came loping towards her position. At first, she thought it was the gleishen shape he had taken in Striden. Then recognition dawned, it was a bear, shaggy and powerful. She stood her ground as it ran at her then through her and was gone in a sparkle of sapphire motes.

There was gasping and coughing. "Help get him on his side." That was her father's voice.

'Enough Maru, drop away,' was Finley's command. She did and felt how heavy her body had become. She swayed. Someone caught her shoulders to keep her from falling to her side.

"They need to rest," said Finley's voice heavily.

"Finley, too," Maru managed to mutter before sinking into oblivion.

* * *

CHAPTER 38

She heard the gulls calling. They were raucously happy about something. She was warm and satisfied. Except a fly or perhaps a stray blade of grass kept brushing her nose and then her cheek. She pushed it away in annoyance and drifted back into the half-wake oblivion of contentment. She rocked gently with the ship.

With the ship! She blinked awake with a start.

Mahew grinned at her with a guilty face. His hand still held the strands of hair he had been teasing against her face. His other arm firmly circled her and held her against him. He kissed her forehead.

"I love you," he said.

Maru thought those the most wonderful words with which to wake. "I love you too." She relaxed into his hold then frowned, "But who are you? Or rather where are you from?"

"Now you ask?" he teased and brushed the strand of hair against her cheek.

"It does not matter," she said, "It was just that when you were dead I realized I knew so little about you."

"And now you want to know it all?" he kissed her again this time on the lips silencing them both.

"Eventually," she said breathlessly as their lips finally parted.

He pulled her closer with his lips fractions from her as he looked her in the eyes with a twinkle of merriment, "Well then, let us see how long we can draw this story out."

Thank you for taking the time to read Shadows. I hope you enjoyed it. Please take the time to leave a review.

OTHER BOOKS BY HELEN MATHEY-HORN:

Laurel: Laurel Goodknight had never had a conventional childhood, despite her parents being proper members of the Bath ton. The only thing that she does well and brings her any sense of worth is painting. When her parents discuss sending her back to... that place, well, she cuts her hair, dons men's clothing and makes a break for London. Accosted on the way by rambunctious young rakes on a lark, she loses the address to the only safe place she knows in London. Contrite for their actions and unaware of her sex the men take Lawrence Godwin under their wing and so begins Laurel's new life. All looks to be fine, except for Beau.

***Dream Warrior**: Teryn knows what the enemy is going to do before they do it. Okay, sometimes is it only minutes before, but usually, there is enough time to pick a path to victory. Until Rabisle. Now, Teryn is on the run with Tasmine, the country's heir, trying to find a place of safety until they can get back to Tasmine's mother, the queen, but at each turn, Rabisle seems to be about one step ahead of them. Teryn may have to use tools even stranger than dream to stop him

***Bait**: What do you do when you come from a family of telepathic warriors, but you lack the telepathic part? Lawren finds a place in a group of off world agents who attempt to 'correct' history, but it turns out although she isn't telepathic, she has charisma in abundance that makes it impossible for her to blend into other cultures. So instead of field work, she is currently in what she considers a dead-end job of teaching new recruits hand-to-hand combat, until someone has a suggestion: go into a violent culture that her bosses haven't had any success at infiltrating as bait to lure out one or possibly two killers.

Dark Queen: Blind from a riding accident, her father dead and her mother remarried to the horrid Mr. Pennington, Cassandra Wyndleigh has few future options and many past secrets. When the dashing Matthew Rowell blackmails her into marriage by threatening to expose those secrets Cassandra agrees, only to find she has given up the devils she knew for the devilish Matthew Rowell and his secrets. Matthew manipulates her in his game. A game in which she does not know the rules or consequences. Is Mr. Andre, Rowell's sincere French friend to be trusted or Mr. Herschell who repeatedly asks her to not trust her husband? And then there are the cards. Each time she is asked to do a tarot reading some evil comes of it. An evil that is centered on the Queen of Spades, the dark queen. How can she face all the secrets and bear silently the worst secret yet?

Olivia: A tired and jaded Major Evert Fulton returns from the Napoleonic Wars to collect an inheritance left to him by his brother. He finds his beautiful sister-in-law, Olivia, has somehow managed to squander her portion leaving her penniless, but extremely proud. How she has accomplished this would seem straightforward considering her extravagant style in clothing and friends and yet is that the truth? And what other secrets hide behind her less than welcoming response to his homecoming?

Uptimers (by Don Horn and Helen Mathey-Horn): A book about people who go back in time to change history until someone from their future tries to write them out of it. So how this time jumping works...you can go backwards in time from anywhere easily, set your co-ordinates and go. But to go forward you have to have someone from the future open a wormhole to you or you use a portable device knowing the date and place (4 pieces of information). When unknown uptimers cut off the one known future access point you have, how do you get uptime and stop them? And to compound the problem that someone in the future is sending more and more assassins back to try and stop you. That can only mean you are getting something right, right? Will you live long enough to find out? Lee Clyburn has lived a long life as an assassin and he's not about to let someone cut it short now.

Nightingale: Rosamund White's deceased father counted on his old friend, Lord Mertheim, to take care of his daughter with his passing. After the funeral, once the creditors had taken the last of the White's earthly possessions, there will still no word from Lord Mertheim. Rose decided to set out for London to go into service. She had done her fair share of hard work during the last few years. She seeks employment at Tittlewell's agency, only as fate would have it, to work as a general-purpose maid at Lord Mertheim's. Maybe now she can find out why she was left with no word for her future and can finally find the safety she had hoped for. Only, Lord Mertheim's will be anything but safe if she doesn't follow the butler's suggestion and stay out of sight.

(*denotes Tienna's World books):